Siostra

Incognito

Part One

Chapter One

The clattering of plates, as they entered the rundown dish washer, rang in my ears as I tried hard to wipe the sweat from my brow.

"Table four is waiting! Stop slacking... if they underpay me it's coming out of your paycheck."

Shouted Crosby. I was coming off of a twelve hour shift, yet no matter how hard I worked it was never hard enough.

His daughter Sally barely did any work yet seemed to be paid triple my salary. It was just a suspicion, she would breeze in and breeze out whenever she pleased yet drove a red Bentley with a white soft top roof.

"Don't worry Daddy, I'll take care of it."

Sally said as she started taking their orders.

"You could learn a lot from my Sally there!"

Crosby said, beaming with pride. She liked to show off for her dad. Whenever he was away from the building she chose to paint her nails and leave everything to me.

Sally wore her bouffant of auburn hair with pride, yet she covered up her freckled covered skin with an inch of foundation. Her rouge was a little too bright, the red wine colour clashed with her vibrant hair yet this didn't deter the male clientele trying it on with her. She could have her pick of the men whilst I tended to blend in with the crowd, partly by choice but even if I could afford all of that war paint I'd put those days behind me.

I had a man who loved me for me, what need did I have to tart myself up? I wanted to avoid attention from others, especially men. The less people knew who I was and what I was doing here the better.

"Thanks Sally."

I said before making my way out of the grotty diner.

"Just where do you think you're going?"

Crosby bellowed. I wish I could just carry on walking and ignore his hideous question but I needed this job. It wasn't easy for an ex prostitute in hiding with no identification, school education or work credentials to offer, to get a job. A fact that Crosby abused gladly.

"It's the end of my shift."

I said quietly. Crosby shook his head fiercely, so much so that his jowls shook like a St Bernard after a long awaited drink of water.

"Not anymore it isn't. I fired Max for stealing and my dish washer is on the fritz so you've been promoted without pay. Sally just had her nails done so you better start washing before I run out of clean dishes."

He said unapologetically, clean may have been optimistic considering how grimy this whole place was. I imagined a world where I could say 'Stick your job where the sun doesn't shine.', what an amazing feeling that would be. But instead I walk back into my thankless, underpaid job without so much as a glare of contempt.

I was supposed to be visiting my man tomorrow and had hoped for at least a couple of hours sleep before I caught the bus up to see him. I guess I'd have to travel straight there in my work uniform now.

"I thought you were going home."

Sally said, without waiting for a response. I pulled up my sleeves and started washing the dishes. I'm not sure how I made it through the next six hours unscathed but I was finally free to visit my beloved.

There was the right way to do things or the wrong way, unfortunately I lived my live by the latter of the two options. I had gone in the wrong direction, whilst ending up with the wrong man, too many times to even count. This time however, I had chosen the moral way of doing things and also the right man; but look where that had landed me.

Poor little Anika Nowak, although people have often called me 'Angel' in the past. A nickname given to me by a man I wish I had never met, the only time I had ever liked hearing it was when Bryan Lambert had said it. I'd managed to make it to my destination in one piece and still awake, it was a close call as I'd nearly fallen asleep on the coach more than a few times.

If it wasn't for the noise the cheap bus made when it opened and closed its doors, I'd likely have dozed off. I was currently sat in a room surrounded by prisoners, I was waiting for the guards to bring my boyfriend in to see me. It had been so long since I had seen him, I felt I may cry upon witnessing Bryan in chains.

Chapter Two

Two guards escorted my boyfriend over to me, they handcuffed him to the table before turning their attentions to me.

"You're his girlfriend?"

One guard asked, the other one returned to his post by the door. An inmate on a neighbouring table, turned around and looked at me in disgust. Normally I'd be preoccupied by the fact that either one of them could have been an old client. Considering the inmates head was shaved and he was sporting a Nazi symbol on his neck, it was safe to say my pale skin was deemed the wrong kind to be mixing with the likes of Bryan.

"You're a disgrace to our race."

The inmate said, as though being a black man meant he somehow was no longer human. He spat on the floor as his face grew even angrier. I had a hundred things I wished to say yet nothing came out. I knew anything I had to say would only pour gasoline onto the fire. The guard decided to intervene.

"There'll be no mixing on my watch. Keep your hands to yourselves and we won't have any trouble."

The guard hovering nearby said, after exchanging a look they both simmered down.

Bryan Lambert was innocent, don't let the black and white striped pyjamas fool you, it was a case of being the wrong colour that had gotten him arrested; alongside choosing to be with the wrong girl. I know you may not trust the word of an ex prostitute, I doubt I would; but I assure you that being black as well as loving me were his *only* crimes.

Me, on the other hand, well I was a criminal through and through, it was Bryan that had made me change my ways (all the good it did him); he was now behind bars fighting for his life. I hadn't chosen a life of crime, some might say it had chosen me. Some might even say that I was a victim, yet no amount of soap could wash away the dirty feeling I had from living my life the way I had.

I seem to be getting ahead of myself, perhaps you're wondering how we got to this point, well for that I will have to take you back to when I was just seventeen years old; a naive little school girl thinking she had all the answers to life. I didn't have a bad upbringing, if that's what you're thinking. I'd had a steady life without much drama, I was just in the wrong place at the wrong time. Much like my beloved had been.

Perhaps we were destined to meet, two unlucky souls who understood each other. It was a day like any other, I had been helping my mum cook our dinner when *they* burst in. I still remember the aroma that filled the air around me as if it was happening right now, my mother loved to cook barszcz just as much as I adored helping her; barszcz was a polish red borscht.

I had heard many stories about the mafia thugs who would terrorise the people in our neighborhood, I had always thought that they were just an urban legend; to keep us in line. Our neighbourhood was filled with immigrants from all walks of life, so it was in our best interests to not disturb the peace.

I was wrong... three thugs breaking our door down kind of wrong. I came to know this as one of the thugs locked me inside of my room. I heard my parents begging for their lives, pleading with the monsters that were now invading our house, my Father screamed as the first gunshot sounded; no noise could be heard after the second.

All was quiet, I heard the shuffling of footsteps amongst mutterings over what to do with me, then my door was opened. The leader out of the three men was rather short but equally wicked, he eyed me up and down whilst telling his men to take me to work in his club. He apparently owned a club where women would dance on poles seducing men so that they would spend money for sexual favours such as lap dances alongside private sessions.

I had heard rumours that some of the women ended up selling themselves for money, I didn't want to become one of these women. I screamed as they hauled me off out of my house. My parents lay dead on the ground in a pool of their own blood. My mother had been clutching her rosary beads in desperation, clearly whoever she was praying to hadn't been listening.

"That is what happens to people who don't pay their debts."

The short man had informed me as they ripped me away from their lifeless bodies.

© created by Scarlet Rivers 31st January 2018

"You will now pay off your parents debts for them."

He added, as if their lives weren't payment enough. I just said nothing so as not to antagonise them, I was already in an awful situation, I certainly didn't want to make things worse for myself.

Originally I was born in Poland, my parents took me to live here in America so that we could have a chance to live a better life. Ironic really, I am sure as they saw the pointed guns in their faces that their choices in life were the first thing to cross their minds. We had run into some financial trouble so out of desperation, without telling any of us, my father went to the mob in order to gain a loan.

Or so I had been told, the men had liked to jeer and taunt me any time they felt I had needed to be put in my place. When my father had been unable to pay them back, I lost the only people in the whole world that I had called family. I had been sitting there thinking of this very incident when the guards had brought Bryan in to see me. Bryan Lambert wasn't just any black guy, he was the love of my life.

"Are you okay? You look like hell."

I stated the obvious as he sat in front of me sporting a freshly applied black eye on his face.

"I'm okay, Anni. How are you coping? Did you speak with the lawyer about the appeal?"

He asked. We had been trying very hard to get him out of prison.

"I have, he wants five thousand dollars before he will be willing to start processing the paperwork. We still owe him money from the last court appearance."

I revealed. I wasn't sure how to get the money without reverting back to my old career; I had my job at Crosby's but after bills I wasn't left with much money.

"It's alright, I will find the money somewhere, I will speak with my business partner."

Bryan said. As I looked into his deep soulful, brown eyes, I thought about the first time that I laid my eyes on this handsome man. I had just turned twenty-five years old, he was visiting the club with his friend from work for his stag do, he had paid for a private lap dance but instead of wanting me to actually give him one, he had just wanted to speak with me.

Bryan had made me feel like a million dollars without even trying hard, he became one of my regulars and I would long for his visits. He begged me to quit, I had wanted to so badly but I had been signed up for a life long service of paying my parents debt off. I was sure after ten years that my debt had finally been paid.

The only time I had ever tried to quit I had landed myself a couple of broken ribs, not to mention the fat lip for the audacity of thinking I would ever be a free woman. Bryan was the one who ended up risking his life to free me, we didn't last long as a couple considering he was arrested less than two years later.

I was sure my previous employer was to blame somehow, I had yet to prove that he was involved in the set up. The mafia had their hands into everything, all it took was a threat or payment in the right place and they could get anything done. I had begged Bryan to run away with me rather than stand trial, he was so sure that because he was innocent that justice would prevail.

He was so naive, it was extremely attractive but definitely not realistic.

"Are you regretting the day you met me?"

I asked.

"Never Anni, I love you."

We weren't able to touch but I could see in his eyes that he had wanted to hold me. His embrace and the memories of our time together was the only thing keeping me going.

Chapter Three

We didn't get much time together, the warden had ordered all of the cell mates to return as visiting hours were officially over. I longed for his kiss, his warm sensual touch, seeing him trapped like a caged animal gave me the worst feeling. He was normally so happy and full of life, whenever I was feeling depressed or alone he would be the first one to comfort me. Now look where we were; I was trying to be the one to comfort him, but our situation seemed too dire to remain positive.

I headed straight to work; I was working twenty-four seven practically, just to make ends meet. Bryan had wanted to pay for everything himself, however now his money had been diverted in order to fund his appeal. I assured him that I was fine on my own, the truth is I had never lived alone before, let alone spend time alone in a bed that had belonged to me.

Most nights I had been with men of every different kind, much to my dismay. Ricardo was the one who used to be in charge of me, he was a scary man, reporting only to the short man who had murdered my parents in cold blood. Most people called him Big Joe, I just called him 'Diabeł' which translated from Polish into English meaning 'the devil'. Diabeł was the only one above Ricardo, although he was a mean son of a bitch I barely ever had to see him.

There was a few occasions that I had been forced to please him sexually due to the nature of my profession, he delighted in reminding me that the gun held to my temple as he raped me was the same weapon that had killed my parents. If I hadn't been so dreadfully terrified of the man I would have grabbed the gun right out of his hand and killed him with it myself, unfortunately I was a complete coward.

This ridiculous need to stay alive was the only reason I hadn't killed myself years ago, I had tried once or twice but something had always held me back. I had been raised Catholic for my entire life leading up to the brutal murder of my parents, they were devout believers who attended Church every Sunday without fail. Ever since I had seen my Mother's rosary beads stained red, drenched in her own blood, the religious aspect of my life hadn't offered me much comfort.

Did I believe in God? I expect so, but after having been raped as many times as I had, God had seemed a little far away in my life. Only after meeting Bryan with his unfaltering belief that God was real (alongside the fact that our meeting had to be divine intervention), did I start to think that maybe, just maybe 'He' could be real. I may have even seen a glimpse of the almighty whilst under the influence of whatever drug cocktail Diabeł had shot me up with after I'd finished servicing him.

I'd never willingly partaken in the drug scene, it seemed to be some sort of game to my captors to see how I'd react whilst under the influence. I'd tried pleading with them to stop yet this only served to amuse them further. I was their toy and they chose to break me any which way they pleased. They took away my dignity as they sold me off to their clients, they trampled on my innocence as they forced me to learn how best to please them. The monsters of the night never truly left me alone, still now they haunt me in my dreams. Faceless creatures that chase me threatening to do all kinds of horrors to me.

There was one time I overdosed, they had to drop me off to the local hospital. Nurses tried questioning how I ended up the way I did but I said nothing, they wouldn't be able to help. In fact I'd likely end up putting them in danger just for knowing how I ended up that way.

"There are people you can talk to, places you can go."

© created by Scarlet Rivers 31st January 2018

One nurse had said. I shook my head, I was planning my escape when I saw Ricardo in the waiting room. There would be no escaping them that night.

"Did your boyfriend get you the drugs?"

The doctor had asked. If only they knew just who that man out there was to me. As much as they seemed intent on getting me to talk, without so much as a peep out of me they eventually gave up. I was surprised they took any interest in me, surely this happens a lot.

"You can't tell Big Joe you were at the hospital."

Ricardo had said as he had hurried me out of there.

It seems that Ricardo had risked his neck to save me, I still don't know why. I assumed he just wanted his moneys worth from me. A piece of me had always thought I'd seen pity in his eyes that night. Clearly prostitutes overdose and die often, but none of them end up at the hospital. Ricardo had given me a false identity, claimed me as his girlfriend to keep them off the scent of my profession.

Most of my days before Bryan had been like that night, it's like I had been placed on a never ending hamster wheel. I had wanted to get off yet I couldn't. The day Bryan helped me escape that horrible existence was a day I'd never forget. Her snuck in and scooped me up in his arms, before I knew what was happening we'd run out if the club and skipped town. I used to spend every waking minute looking over my shoulder.

I had just begun settling to the idea that we might have gotten away with it, until Bryan was arrested unjustly. If anyone was my saviour, I think it would be him. I never wished on a rosary bead that things would improve, I was in hell when Bryan took me to heaven. I wasn't actually sure there was enough Hail Mary's in the entire world that could atone for my sins. I have had every orifice of my body violated by varying colours and types of penis's, Men had become a blur to me without even having a face as they touched me.

Chapter Four

I had learnt to block out all the pain and distress that went along with the profession of 'pole dancer'. Some men were gentle, but more commonly they saw me as a piece of meat to be toyed with. Pleasure had never ever been a factor related to sex until Bryan had come into my life, I still remember the ecstasy over my very first orgasm. So if anyone deserves to be behind bars it's me, not my beloved. He deserved the highest honour for giving me those two years of peace.

I shelved all of the nice feelings that memories of Bryan brought to my life as I entered the diner.

"Anika, where have you been? We needed you over ten minutes ago."

Crosby complained. My boss seemed to forget that I wasn't even supposed to be in for this shift, I had agreed to do it as a favour for his daughter Sally. He also chose not to acknowledge the fact I had only left my last shift less than eight hours ago. I hadn't even had the chance to sleep properly, return to my house, freshen up or stop to eat or drink.

"Sorry Crosby, traffic was a nightmare."

I said, a lame excuse I know. Crosby had an extreme personality, he was a 'larger than life' kind of guy, in every sense of the word. As much as his personality would fill a room, so would he, his gut was protruding out of the top of his trousers as if it were trying to escape. His chef hat was stained with grease from the fryer and his hairy belly button could be seen right through the buttonholes of his once white tunic.

I couldn't judge too much considering I had slept at a bus station just so I wouldn't miss the coach up to the prison, I had been wearing my uniform for more than forty-eight hours. I'd worry about my body aroma if it wasn't for the fact the diner itself smelled like a month old dripping tray. Crosby's full name was Harold Walter

Crosby the second, but he preferred to be summoned using his surname; he thought it sounded authoritative.

Crosby was the proud owner of this shoddy excuse for a diner, I along with two other waitresses was the entire of his staff; I can't even be sure when the last time his place had a decent clean. I don't think that it was up to code, it certainly wouldn't pass any kind of health and hygiene tests, however his brother worked as a Health Inspector so had managed to pull some strings on his behalf.

"Quit standing there and get to work before I have a mind to fire your skinny ass."

Crosby insisted whilst staring at me, sweat dripped from his brow as he wheezed his commanding words in my direction. I didn't need to be told twice, I grabbed my apron and started taking empty trays to the kitchen.

It was a far better job than the last one I had, I hadn't needed any kind of reference to work here which was a rarity to say the least. I would take eighteen hour shifts of grumpy customers, complaining about the standard of food that they were receiving, over anal sex any day of the week. Although some clients would demand I partake in whichever drug they had interest in, that would at least take some pain away; it helped me block out the memory easier too.

I had been hooked on more than one kind of drug whilst working for Ricardo, it had helped take the edge off of what I was having to do each night. I still remember the first time clear as day, Ricardo had been the first one of my 'clients'. My first in every respect of the word, actually. He had explained at the time that he had to 'show me the ropes' of my new profession, he had taken my virginity away, we had sex every night for over a week so that he could let me experience first hand what was to be expected of me.

I had fought him for the first few days which led to him beating the crap out of me, he would just say that it was good experience for me because whatever the client wants, the client gets. If a man wanted to beat me instead of fuck me then that's what I was there for, I quickly learnt to submit; it hurt less when I didn't resist. Although that first traumatic week had caused pain I may never recover from, not just physical but it was a trauma like no other. I had a lot of hate to go around but Ricardo had the lions share of it most days, other days Big Joe won that honour.

There was nothing enjoyable about any of it, the dancing was hard work let alone having to serve punters their drinks half nude. If they grabbed me without paying first they were taught a lesson by Ricardo, but as soon as that green was shown I was fair game. Crystal had shown me the ropes of how to perform on the pole, how to lap dance along with learning all of the ways to stay afloat in this nasty world. She had been kicked to the curb the second she had turned thirty-five, they had said that she was too old then threw her out of the club like a piece of garbage.

Not too long after that she wound up DOA at the local hospital, she had jacked herself up with so much heroine that she was dead before the paramedics had arrived. I know this because I was the one who had called them. I went to go see her after begging Ricardo to let me go, only to find her pale corpse waiting for me. I was naive enough to think that she could still be saved, she had died hours before I had even got there.

Crystals real name had been Jenifer, she had been my one and only ally in this cruel world I'd been dragged into. She was an orphan from a young age and had been fending for herself on the streets until Big Joe 'saved her'. She was given a roof over her head and a dangerous entourage, in a way I guess she saw it as her home. I would have called her my friend but it did you no favours having friends in that world, friends and family made you vulnerable. A rule Crystal had taught me early on.

I guess you could say we had been surrogate sisters, or at least she was the closest thing I'd ever had to one. Crystal didn't know how to be anything other than what she had become, when she wasn't able to do it anymore she saw only one way out. Crystal had been braver than I. She didn't have anyone, outside of that group of thugs who had recruited her, in a way I was lucky to have one lifeline in Bryan. After my long shift at the diner had ended I aimed to go straight home to sleep, only I never made it home that night.

Chapter Five

Whilst unconscious I had slipped off into dreamland quite happily, Bryan and I were dancing to our favourite song as I rested my head upon his shoulder; he was singing the tune softly to me. My skin paled in comparison to his, it was as if milk lay next to spilled coffee with my hand against his.

We would often get passers by staring at us as if we didn't belong together, they would scoff while saying things like 'couldn't find any of your own colour then?' or 'Milk and oil aren't meant for mixing'. I loved his tone of skin colour, no one would ever make me feel bad about loving a man of colour. Big Joe had been opposed to our union, he didn't like him always coming to the club in order to see me.

He had warned me that if I were to ever leave him, especially for a black guy, that he would make us both pay. Voices could be heard as I came to, I recognised them instantly, Big Joe was talking with Ricardo about me. Ricardo wanted to give me a warning while Big Joe wouldn't be satisfied unless I was made to suffer for my transgressions.

I had much preferred my dreamland to the reality I now faced, as I glanced down I saw my hands tied up with rough string to the arms of a metal chair. My head felt like it had been hit with a ton of bricks, the six foot four man who I knew only by the name 'Bone Crusher' was staring right at me.

"Hey Boss, the bitch is waking up."

One of Big Joes foot soldier's informed him. Big Joe and Ricardo both shut up as they looked towards where I was sitting, Ricardo stayed where he was while Big Joe headed towards me. His mouth opened wide enough for me to see his gold tooth gleam at me, he had long black wavy, greasy hair which had been covered up by a black fedora on his head.

With his skin tone being light brown alongside his clothes being completely black, the only colour that could be seen was a red stripe across his hat. He was the image of a dark soul come to life which was why I always called him Diabeł. I wasn't sure what dark crevice this man had existed in before coming to torment me, but I knew he wasn't born here. His accent was just as thick as that fateful day we met.

He muttered under his breath in some foreign dialect I didn't recognise, there was a high chance it was Spanish. If I had to guess I'd say he came from Mexico. Many rumours swilled around these parts but he enjoyed the air of mystery alongside the element of fear it brought to people, not knowing his origin story. I couldn't imagine something this evil being born into this world. I'm sure he was the devil reincarnated somehow.

"So, *princess,* you have woken up now."

He gripped my face so that I would be forced to look him in the eyes

"I am going to kill you, that way you can earn your name 'Angel' back again. Although, I'm not so sure heaven will take a whore."

Big Joes words were like venom spilling from his rotting gums. His sinister laugh echoed in the room as 'Bone

Crusher' joined in, Ricardo just stood there, at the back of the room, looking very unamused.

"Just let the bitch go, she is no use to us, she has passed the age requested by our punters."

Big Joe let go of my face turning his attention back to Ricardo as they began to row again.

My thoughts were only of Bryan.

"You can do anything you want to me…"

I started saying. As if whatever they had planned hadn't already been done to me.

"…just let Bryan go free."

I pleaded. With that I got a hefty, back handed slap across my cheek from Diabeł.

"Did I give you permission to speak, *whore*? Don't worry your black boy will get what's coming to him. It's such a shame you won't live to see the torture he will go through. I will make sure he pleads for death before I finally grant him that request, he will know you are the cause of his suffering before he finally passes to the next life."

He said. Hate was rife in his eyes. Diabeł nodded at 'Bone Crusher', he gleefully grabbed hold of my hand getting ready to snap one of my fingers in half. He snapped my pinky finger and searing pain filled every inch of my body. I refused to utter a sound as I pinched my eyes tightly and forced in a scream.

Bone Crusher laughed loudly, his noisy laugh could knock down a small building.

"Why no scream. Being brave won't save you."

Said Bone Crusher. He was practically a giant, his hug could snap me in two without even trying. He too had an accent but it was far less exotic. I recognised a few words he'd said in his language in the past. He was from some part of Russia but I'd never bothered to ask him for confirmation.

"Please… stop… I'm pregnant."

I said through gritted teeth, still fighting through the pain. I kept my eyes clenched whilst waiting for more pain to take over me but nothing happened, I opened my eyes only to see Bone Crusher shaking his head back and forth.

"Bone Crusher don't break pregnant woman."

He said to Big Joe. With that he pulled his hand away refusing to lay another finger on me. Bone Crusher was more like hired help than a foot soldier, he was called in for big jobs but wasn't there day to day. Clearly I was worth shelling out the big bucks for.

"She is probably just lying to save herself, just break something of hers now!"

Big Joe shouted in venomous anger, but Bone Crusher just refused to touch me.

Diabeł headed straight towards me when the click of a gun being ready to fire could be heard, everyone stood still as they turned around to see Ricardo with a gun to Big Joe's head.

"I said let the bitch go, she has paid her debts, I made sure of it. What use is she to me now, pregnant? Fuck that."

Ricardo said. Big Joe moved in closer to Ricardo's gun.

"You don't have the balls!"

Big Joe said before flashing his gold tooth. Without even flinching Ricardo shot the gun, a loud bang could be heard as the blood from his head wound splattered onto his face. He spat on his body after it had hit the ground, his fedora rolled of his head; the expression of surprise was etch on his dead face.

"Rest in peace you piece of shit!"

Ricardo said sarcastically as he wiped the blood from his face. I was in shock.

I never ever thought that Ricardo would have stood up to Diabeł like that, not in a million years. Yet here we were.

"What we are doing with pregnant whore?"

Bone Crusher asked, he didn't seem phased by what had just happened. Ricardo finished wiping the brain matter from his face as he looked at me.

"She won't talk if she knows what's good for her, let her go. I got no use for a pregnant old wench like her."

Ricardo said after a brief pause. I looked at this once handsome man standing before me, when he had first violated me he had been younger with toned muscles.

Over the years he had aged ungracefully, he had a scrawny appearance alongside a receding hairline. Two of his teeth were now missing, I had no idea why he felt compelled to save me from death but I was grateful all the same. At the time of his attentions towards me I had loathed him but over the years he had been good to me, as far as a pimp could have ever been 'good' to his prized whore.

He looked after his girls so long as they were well behaved, he had seen me escape that night with Bryan but hadn't stopped me. Bone Crusher shoved a hood over my face as he untied me, the next thing I knew I was being hauled into the boot of a car. We drove a short distance before I was released, the car drove off while the hood was still on my head. I removed it slowly, unsure of where they had taken me, I seemed to have been dropped in the same place that they had clobbered me over the head in the first place.

I went on home, I didn't have anywhere else to go, it isn't easy keeping friends in the business that I had gotten myself caught up in. I listened to the voicemail messages on my machine, I had missed a call from Bryan, he was being released. Some new evidence had been found at the crime scene which now proved his innocence, I knew he had been set up; Ricardo must have been behind his release. I quickly showered then changed so that I could go meet him up at the prison.

I tied my hair back to cover up the wound on my head and strapped my broken finger up to straighten it; I could always go to hospital after I had collected him. They had hit me pretty hard over the head, I would probably need stitches or something and my finger would heal eventually. It wasn't the first broken bone I'd received, but I was hoping it would be my last. I opened the door ready to leave when I was surprised by a familiar face, Bryan was there in front of me.

Chapter Six

I stood there in shock, he lifted me into the air and spun me around which only served to make me woozy. It could have been the head wound or the baby.

"I missed you so much, Anni."

Bryan said whilst he twirled me around, thankfully he put me down a minute later. He was lying me down onto the couch, kissing me passionately when he noticed my

© created by Scarlet Rivers 31st January 2018

injured hand. Before he began asking me a hundred questions I decided to let the cat out of the bag.

"I have something to tell you…"

I started saying, I wasn't sure how he was going to take the news. I paused as he lifted his face up, he held my gaze and began looking deeply into my eyes.

"…I'm pregnant."

I announced. He looked confused for a minute before joy spread across his face. I had initially thought that he may have been unhappy about the news, I hadn't wanted to tell him while he was in prison. I'd found out only a week after he had been incarcerated.

I was sure he had been searching my eyes for betrayal, I recognised distrust in his eyes as he noticed my injury; he'd had the slightest concern that I had gone back to selling myself.

"Are you serious Anni? How? I mean it's mine, right? That's amazing, how far gone are you?"

He asked. I was a little annoyed he would doubt it would be anyone else's but considering how we met I let it slide. I showed him the scan picture.

"Of course it's yours, I found out a couple of months back but you had just been arrested and I didn't want to tell you until I passed the twenty week scan. I had it last week, I'll be twenty-one weeks on Sunday. I was going to tell you yesterday but after I saw the bruises, and how that inmate was threatening us, well I didn't want to rock the boat."

I revealed. Tears were in his eyes as he looked at the sonogram picture, he turned to look at me but had noticed the gash on my head.

"Anni is that blood? What's going on? You've injured your hand, there's blood on your neck... is that a bruise on your face?"

Bryan asked. He went to touch my head but I winced, I pulled my long blonde hair down for him to see clearly. He examined my injuries a little closer.

Bryan stroked my face where Big Joe had struck me, we had matching bruises now.

"Your head is going to need stitches. Who did this to you?"

He asked. I shook my head in reply.

"It doesn't matter, it's over now"

I replied. Bryan looked like he might explode.

"It was Diabel, wasn't it?"

Bryan asked. I nodded briefly.

"I'm going to go kick the shit into him, he has no right coming after us. I paid for you fair and square."

He revealed. His words stung.

"*Paid* for me?"

I asked, feeling more than a little hurt. His face fell as he realised what he had said.

"Look, it's not what you think. I gave Ricardo five grand to look the other way and keep that monster from coming after you. I didn't want you to know because I thought you would take it the wrong way."

He replied. I grew a little angry.

"What way could I take it? I was just a purchase to you, a business transaction."

I shouted. I tried really hard to contain my rage but after the night I had endured I couldn't pretend to be okay with this.

I started getting ready for work. I was going to call in sick so I could meet Bryan at the prison but seeing as he was here, safe and sound, I used the excuse to get out of the house. I was busy trying to wipe the dried blood in my hair when he came in.

"Anni, you're the love of my life. I didn't buy you, I don't own you. If you had wanted to run away from me and never come back I wouldn't regret spending that money. I just wanted you to be free. I lucked out when I found out you really loved me."

He said. I had stopped being angry but his confession had really struck a nerve.

"He's dead."

I replied after an awkward silence. Bryan looked at me in horror, he must have thought that I had been the one to end his life. I had always wondered what it would be like to see the life end of the person who had killed my parents, it wasn't joy I felt but a hollow emptiness instead.

"It wasn't me, they kidnapped me and were going to kill me. Ricardo shot Diabel then set me free, I think he also gave in the evidence that released you. We have our dear friend

Bone Crusher to thank for my broken pinky finger."

I said.Bryan sat back down

"Let's get you to the hospital Anni, you need your head looked at."

Bryan said, his concern for my well being was touching. I hated going to the hospital but at least with him by my side it will be bearable.

Chapter Seven

I let Bryan look after me, it was nice to see how much he cared. He drove me to hospital, making sure that I was seen to promptly and with great care. Due to the colour of his skin he was often treated as badly as me, that was until he let them know who he was. Bryan was a partner of a prestigious business however he wasn't the face of the company, his white step brother was. The name Bryan Lambert carried weight at this hospital especially, his company was responsible for their new children's wing.

I felt as if he were my knight in shining armour, he rarely saw the prostitute in me. To him I was this innocent girl whom he loved unconditionally, ever since he rescued me I'd been free to live my life. The nurse stitched up my head, giving me some medical advice on how to look after my injury along with instructions for Bryan on what to look out for in case I had a concussion. No questions were asked about how I'd broken my finger, they taped it up and offered me some pain killers which I refused.

Bryan drove me back to my apartment, he had to sell his flat when they froze his assets in order to pay for the lawyer.

"In the morning we are moving into a much better place Anni, I can't believe you have been living here in this awful apartment."

Bryan announced. We had been living together in his fancy dwelling before he had been sentenced to life in prison, they had accused him of murder in the first degree. It was a con, Bryan didn't even know the man he had supposedly killed, I had recognised him as one of Big Joe's cronies.

I knew it was a setup but I had no way of proving it in court, I had been made to watch in agony as they dragged him away into a place filled with criminals, knowing he hadn't done a thing wrong.

"This was all I could afford."

© created by Scarlet Rivers 31st January 2018

I reminded him as we entered my poky flat. Bryan kissed me, how I had missed his sensual tongue caressing my own, I yearned to feel him inside of me once more. Before I even knew it we were naked together, embracing in a passion I had only ever felt when with him, he knew just how to stir up my senses and cause me to lose all of my inhibitions.

"I love you, Bryan."

I said and indulged myself in a pleasurable orgasm. This just caused the fire inside of him to stir as he changed positions and entered inside of me once more, it was as if the beast had been unleashed.

All that pent up energy over the last few months away from me were all coming out in that one moment. I trusted him beyond all reason, I knew he would never hurt me or force me in any sexual way so with him I was free to enjoy his naked body pressed against mine. As he reach completion his body relaxed.

"I love you too, Anni."

He whispered in my ear. Bryan kissed me again before falling asleep in my arms, I too joined him as we slept completely nude in each other's arms.

It wasn't about sex when it came to our relationship, we were both quite closed off when it came to discussing it, but when we were in bed together we most certainly became of one mind. Bryan didn't ever like to hear about my past sexual encounters, he knew how men had treated me and it turned his stomach to hear about it. There was a sorrow in his eyes anytime I would mention things from my past, he accepted it for the most part but there were limitations on how much he could understand me.

As much as he could empathise to the horrors I had experienced, he had no idea what it was like to be inside my head. Bryan was everything to me, I knew our life together wouldn't exactly be easy due to the race difference, but the added annoyance of my past constantly trying to get the better of us was making things more difficult. It was frowned upon in my neighbourhood for white to be with black let alone to have a kid together. I had suggested that we move to a more accepting environment but he had his company, he also said that wherever it was that we might go there would always be someone against us. I didn't want to raise a child in a racist neighbourhood, I would need to broach the subject again as soon as I was able to.

In the morning I had to wake up extra early to go for another grinding shift at the diner, Crosby would not be happy if I was late again. He can't have been happy that Bryan called in sick for me yesterday. It was hard enough to get that crummy job, let alone have to find another one while pregnant. Bryan had tried to convince me to stay in bed, I just reminded him that he had to get into work just the same as I did. Just because he was a free man it didn't mean that the world was going to stop, I kissed him then left after a quick shower.

I looked at myself in the mirror stroking my tummy, it hadn't grown enough to see it while wearing clothes but while I was naked you could see a slight pudge to my womb area; one that hadn't been there before. I had felt the baby move inside of me, it was like tiny little swirling movements. My face had a little colour to it from the brutal slap from the now deceased villain Diabeł, I used makeup to cover the slight bruising, I also pulled my hair back in order to cover my head injury. My hand was a little harder to hide but I'm sure I could excuse it away.

My washed out diner uniform made me look hideous, Bryan always found me attractive but even he would be the first to admit how unflattering this uniform was. My beloved was fast asleep snoring as I left the cruddy apartment heading to my job, the sun had only just begun to poke it's head out when I ran to get the bus. I was wearing a thick coat along with my comfortable work shoes, they were similar to the ones nurse's would wear on a long shift, considering I would be on my feet for over twelve hours at a time they were very much a requirement in my life. While Bryan was in prison I had a customer who was a nurse, she was wearing the exact same shoes to me which had sparked up a conversation.

The lady had mentioned a course that she had done in order to learn how to be a nurse, she had given me her business card, it was a college who takes on students of all ages alongside people who can't always afford the full tuition up front. I must have emanated a 'poor vibe', I still had the card and had been considering nursing as a profession. It wasn't exactly the best of times to change careers but it was something I was strongly considering, once I'd had the baby of course. My age was also a factor, not many people my age were starting a career from scratch.

It would be nice to be in a profession where you could save people's lives instead of watch them take a beating, I knew all about how to hurt people from watching Ricardo over the years; learning about how to stop the bleeding instead of causing it would be a nice change of scenery. I wanted to make my child proud of their Mum, I hadn't been any sort of role model previously in my life but I intended on being one now.

Crosby was waiting for me as I opened the front door.

"About time you showed up."

He said. Even when I was on time he still had to moan.

"I'm here now aren't I?"

I replied in kind. I didn't mind his grumpy demeanour, he was harmless.

"I assume your hand is why you didn't show yesterday."

He said as he noticed my injury.

"A cyclist slammed into me."

I lied. He furrowed his brow.

"Look it's not my business and your boyfriend paid me handsomely for the loss of staff yesterday but you shouldn't put up with a man that beats on you."

He said. I don't know what surprised me more, the fact Bryan had paid for the pleasure of my company and not told me yet again or the fact Crosby actually cared about my welfare.

"That Negro might be a big deal in this town but it's still not right."

He added, making me realising it was likely just his race that bothered him more than the fact he thought he was a woman beater.

"It wasn't him, I promise."

I replied. He straightened himself up and returned to his former grizzly self.

"Table five needs you."

He replied gruffly. With that I was off to serve the customers. I was surprised to see the nurse who had given me the business card was the one sat waiting for some service.

"Hi, again. Last time didn't scare you off clearly."

I teased. The nurse just looked up at me blankly, obviously I hadn't made that much of an impression on her from our first meeting. She all of a sudden noticed my shoes when recognition hit her face like a thunderbolt.

"Oh, hey, shoe twin."

She said. I had been labelled, it wasn't the worst name I had been called so I rolled with it.

"That's me, your 'shoe twin'. What can I get you?"

I asked. I had seen Crosby's eyes peering at me.

He didn't like people who dilly dallied.

"Just a coffee, Hun. Did you think about enrolling into the nursing programme? I think you would make a great nurse."

She asked. It felt nice to be treated as a real person, for too long I'd felt as if even pets had been placed above me in the food chain of life.

"I'm not sure on the timing right now…"

I started saying. By now Crosby was glaring at me so I chose to end the conversation.

"… I'll be right back with that coffee."

I said, scurrying off to fix a cup of hot joe for the friendly nurse.

"There are other customers who need service!"

Crosby complained. I hurried as fast as I could to bring my customer her order. As I plonked the cup of coffee on her table I smiled briefly before getting the orders from the other tables who were waiting.

Once the coffee cup was nearly empty I went back over to offer her a refill.

"Do you want another?"

I asked. She sat there reading her book, deep in thought as she answered me.

"No I'm fine, I have a shift in twenty minutes. Congratulations by the way."

She said without looking at me. I turned back to her feeling a little perplexed, she finally lifted her head out of her book.

"On the baby."

She whispered as she gestured to my stomach. I became flustered, I began looking around to make sure Crosby hadn't seen her. My face was as red as Sally's lips.

"Don't worry… Anika, is it? I won't say a thing."

The lady had read my badge before calling me by name, my cheeks felt warm as I became confused. How did she know?

"Um… yes…"

I started saying before looking over my shoulder.

"…how did you know?"

I whispered back to her.

"I am a nurse after all, clearly you can't talk here. Call me after your shift finishes, my name is Gabriela."

Gabriela said. She smiled kindly as she passed me her card but this time it had her personal number on it too.

"Thank You."

I said, clearing her cup away as soon as she got up to leave; I didn't fancy another lecture from Crosby today.

Chapter Eight

I had finally reached home but it was rather late, the only thing I had been interested in doing was getting into bed so I could sleep. My day had been challenging to say the least; I had been the only one in, aside from a cantankerous Crosby, throughout the day. Sally had made plans with her girlfriends, Crosby fired his newest employee which meant I had to wash, dry and take orders.

As I reached my shoddy abode Bryan greeted me, he had just finished running me a hot bubble bath, it was just what I needed to soothe my aching muscles. Once I had completed my bath I then got dressed so that I could join Bryan on the sofa.

"I have something to ask you Anni."

Bryan said as he cosied up to me, looking at me with barely contained excitement.

"Will you marry me?"

He asked, this question stunned me into silence. I took a long look at the beautiful diamond ring in front of me.

"Well, say something, beautiful… don't hold me in suspense."

He said after an awkwardly long silence. I grinned from ear to ear, there was only one answer on my mind.

"YES!"

I shouted, grabbing the ring I placed it on my wedding finger before he had the chance to change his mind.

I sat there looking at my hand, it looked so elegant draped in such finery.

"It fits perfectly."

I revealed. We kissed to seal the deal. I felt as though I should pinch myself to make sure that it wasn't just a dream, things in my life hadn't ever been this good before. I was so excited about the ring that I had nearly forgotten to call the nurse that I had met, I quickly let Bryan know all about the conversation that we had shared back at the diner. I was a little surprised by his reaction to my enthusiasm for nursing.

"*You,* a nurse?"

Bryan said whilst scoffing unapologetically, his expression made it sound much worse.

"I think I would make a good nurse."

I said a little defensively, his giggles felt condescending as I continued trying to justify myself.

"She also thought I would make an *amazing* nurse, in fact I am going to call her right now."

I said, he gestured towards the phone. I picked up the phone, ready to dial, as I looked back at his continued amusement.

Why on earth couldn't I be a nurse? Was it so far fetched to think that I could be anything other than a lady of the night? I was more than my past and I was determined to prove it, people may only see an old washed up hooker when they look at me. I just hoped that wasn't all Bryan saw me as. I was going to change everyone's perception of me, even if it was the last thing that I did. I picked up the receiver on the phone, as I dialed the digits on the card in front of me my hand shook nervously.

"Hello is this Gabriela?"

I asked. There was a female voice on the other end of the phone.

"Yes, who is this?"

She replied.

"It's Anika, we met a couple of times at Crosby's Diner."

I said. Before I could say much else her shriek rang in my ears.

"Anika! I am so glad you rang me. I have great news, let's meet up for a coffee."

She said rather loudly.

"Great, where can I meet you? I am off until tomorrow afternoon."

I revealed. Gabriela hummed a little as she rustled papers on her side of the phone before replying.

"Okay fabulous, I shall meet you at ten. Do you know where Rosie's Cafe is?"

She asked. I did know where that was, in fact it was Crosby's biggest rival.

"I do, I am just a little worried about showing up there."

I said. I didn't want to be spotted by someone who knew I worked with Crosby.

"It will be fine, got to go now, bye bye."

She said finally, with that she hung up the phone. When I turned back around Bryan was heavily engrossed with his newspaper; I hated reading the news, there was never any *good* news.

They only ever seemed to go on and on about the terrible things that were going on in the world, yet never told of the horrors that people like me had to endure. Considering the fact that I had lived in the worst sort of circumstances I wanted to immerse myself in the good of this world as opposed to the bad. It was the only way I stayed a float in this terrible world. Anything could set off another one of my episodes.

I'm not sure what set me off this time, it was either how dismissive Bryan had been over my dreams or perhaps it was the fact he paid for my time yesterday. I'm not sure what set my mind down the dark path that led to memory lane yet I found myself there all the same. I began to feel dirty, I saw blood on the floor then on my hands.

I tried closing my eyes knowing I was just seeing things but nothing I did made the feeling go away. I felt as though my skin was on fire, I began scratching furiously. I headed to the shower being sure to place my beautiful ring somewhere safe, I lathered the soap all over my body trying hard to scrub off the unclean feeling, I never seemed to feel clean despite my daily wash.

I was constantly reminded of incidents from my past, the memories haunted me, as time went on they became further away but never far enough to forget completely. Memories were hitting me like a flood as I drew blood. I'd scrubbed too hard and tore my skin. I didn't notice at first, in fact I had assumed it was just my mind playing tricks on me and had chosen to ignore it despite the searing pain I was now feeling.

I tried hard to force down every bad memory deep down inside of me, I crouched on the floor letting the shower wash my blood down the drain. I trailed off into the depths of my mind and became lost in bad memory after bad memory; the sight of blood had taken me to my worst one. I'd begun scrubbing a different patch of skin and seemingly forgot I was even scrubbing until the skin began to rip away from my arm again.

The pain shocked me back to reality for just a moment but as I saw the blood washing away in the shower, the flood of red just brought me back to a flashback of my parents death, they felt nearly close enough to touch as I shouted.

"Mamo, Ojcze, proszę obudź się."

It was polish for 'Mother, Father, please wake up.', I had thought at the time that maybe they were just unconscious. I hadn't realised I was shouting, this memory was the one I avoided at all costs. Yet here I was in the shower wishing the image now plaguing me would go away. I was curled up in a ball with my eyes firmly shut begging for my mind to release me from this agony.

There had been no reply to my plea as they'd dragged me out of my house, all the kicking and screaming in the world wouldn't have stopped them from taking me. As I sat, helpless in the shower, Bryan came in to check on me.

"Darling, are you Okay? You have been in here for ages. I thought you already had a bath, why is the shower on?"

Bryan asked, perhaps my shouting had distracted him from his paper. I could hear his voice but I was unable to respond, I was frozen in that moment.

"Mamo, Ojcze, proszę obudź się."

I whispered.

"Anni, come back to me Anni."

Bryan said, he had seen me like this before. Bryan climbed into the shower fully clothed as he turned off the water and carried me out of their fully naked and dripping wet.

Grabbing a towel he wrapped it around me, holding me as if I were the weight of a feather in his arms.

"Mamo, Ojcze, proszę obudź się."

I said again, he dressed the sores on my arm then turned his attentions back to me, he began stroking my face.

"Come back to me my love, please Anni, it's me Bryan. I love you."

He said as he kissed me gently on my lips, pulling me in tightly, as he held me up I looked into his eyes, something about his face seemed to always bring me back into reality. I broke down and sobbed like a small child.

"Shh… it's alright Anni… It's all over now. They can't touch you now. No one can touch you ever again, you're safe now."

He said gently whilst drying the tears away from my eyes.

"They were so still and lifeless, I should have helped them. If I was a nurse maybe I could have saved them, maybe I would still have parents. My friend Crystal might be alive today if I were trained."

I confessed. In that moment Bryan finally understood what nursing meant to me, I didn't even know why it meant so much to me until that moment. I guess I had always blamed myself for those deaths, despite the fact no one could have saved them.

"If you want to be a nurse, than you shall be a nurse. You can be anything you want to be my beautiful fiancé."

He said as he placed my engagement ring back on my finger, he must have picked it up when he carried me in.

"You really scared me."

Bryan admitted.

"Sorry."

I said as I snuggled into his strong manly shoulders, it was then that I noticed his wet clothes.

"I'm also sorry for getting you wet."

I said. Bryan laughed then he kissed me tenderly.

"Maybe you can help me get out of my wet clothes."

He said as he scooped his hand inside of my towel, cupping my breast, I quickly unbuttoned his shirt while he undid his belt as if it were a race.

Before long we were both naked on the floor, his stiff member felt so smooth against my delicate palm. I wrapped my legs around his back as he placed his hard penis inside of me, I wanted him so badly. As he made love to me I felt so close to him, I didn't want it to ever end. No one could touch me the way he did, he touched my soul deep inside of me, as our bodies became one right there on the carpet he was the only thing in my mind.

The nasty memories of the past shifted back to where they belonged, way deep down inside of me. What may have only lasted for a manner of minutes felt as though it had gone on for an eternity

"I love you Bryan."

I said, we kissed as he reached completion.

This beautiful man was all mine, he loved me unconditionally, it was such a warming feeling to know that he was there for me. After we had gotten dressed we sat in each other's arms silently, I stared at my ring that had been placed on my finger once again while he looked at the TV. Bryan glanced at me then back to the TV.

"I think you should do the nursing course, I can help you pay for it."

He said. I squeezed him in delight.

"Thank You for believing in me."

I replied. Bryan kissed my head ending the perfect day, nothing could top that moment.

Chapter Nine

Bryan had left for work early yet I wasn't working until late, which allowed me to sleep in. For the first time in a long time I had a restful night; I slept straight through and didn't even hear him leave. He had been looking into getting another flat for us, there was one that he'd wanted me to take a look at for him as it wasn't too far away from where I was meeting Gabriela.

I had complained about the price but he would hear none of it, I always felt as if I should be contributing more money than I was to our way of living. He saw himself as the 'breadwinner' so it didn't matter to him how much I was earning or not earning, I honestly think he would prefer me to stay at home instead of working. I could never be a kept woman, I needed to feel useful, to feel as if I contributed to the relationship.

I met the realtor outside of the property, I was right on time at nine. Despite this fact the man seemed to be in a hurry.

"Right this way."

He said without introducing himself. I followed him into the elevator where I was met with silence the whole ride up.

"The building seems clean."

I said, by this stage I was just filling dead air.

"Hmmm."

He said in reply before muttering something under his breath. He was an attractive guy, perhaps in his mid forties. His face seemed familiar but I wasn't keen on finding out why.

"Right this way."

He said again as he went to unlock the front door.

The flat was nice, much better than the one we were in at the moment, there was no furniture in it at all yet. It was just like a blank canvas, the place felt open while the view was somewhat to be desired due to the fact that the window was overlooking a construction site. Aside from that one minor and temporary flaw the place was perfect, I could picture us sitting in the spacious living room area before putting the baby down to sleep in the second room.

"I'll ask my fiancé to get in touch."

I said after completing the tour in silence.

"*Fiancé?*"

He said in disgust. I grew a little annoyed, I was used to getting abuse for all different reasons but this guy was getting on my nerves.

"Look, who are we hurting? I love him and he loves me, why should it matter what colour our skin is? Our child will share both our skin tones and I'll love that child just the same!"

I said in protest. He scoffed in reply.

"You think this is about the colour of your skin? I'm Jennifer's boyfriend or at least I was before she killed herself!"

He blurted out. I realised where I knew him from now. He was a regular of Crystals, one of her favourite clients.

"Why should you get a happy ending? Crystal died because of you! She stuck her neck out for you and it got her killed. I mean engaged? With a kid on the way? Where is the justice in that?"

He added. Now I was really confused.

"I don't understand why you're blaming me, I was devastated the day my friend died. I rang the ambulance... I was the one who tried to save her..."

I started saying, but he just shook his head whilst holding in tears.

"That night you had her cover for you, when you so desperately needed to see your precious fiancé... Big Joe found out and kicked her out of the club. You're the reason she lost her job and any way of making money! She came to me pleading for some cash and I gave it to her but she used it to buy enough drugs to kill herself!"

He said. I looked at his wedding ring and grew annoyed.

"It's not like you are blameless, I mean supplying her drug money... I should be mad at _you_! Or maybe your wife was the priority."

© created by Scarlet Rivers 31st January 2018

I said as I gestured to the gold band handcuffing his finger.

"You're right, I tried to leave my wife but she's mentally ill. My money goes to her medical bills. We lost a baby many years ago, she was still born. They look after her for me but at a cost, I couldn't afford to run away with Jenifer but everyday I regret giving her that money. I should have used it to buy her a bus ticket to anywhere but here."

He revealed. In that moment I knew he wasn't angry at me, not really. I recognise that look of guilt and shame in his eyes because it reflected in my own.

"I loved Crystal like a sister, I had no idea that's why she lost her job... I'm so sorry. I'm also sorry for judging you so quickly too."

I said. He wiped tears out of his eyes.

"I blame myself already."

I added. He gave me half a smile.

"I loved her, I know it's not your fault. I'm just so angry. I miss her still."

He said. He managed to compose himself, he cleared his throat before speaking.

"So, I'll wait for Bryan's call."

He said.

"She really liked you, I never knew your real name but Crystal called you her honey pot."

I said as he was walking off, he turned around and gave me a big grin.

"She called me that because I was her sugar daddy but she always liked honey in her tea instead of sugar. My name is Terence, I actually didn't know your name was Anika until today. I

always thought Angel was a wrong fit for you but now I see it. I'm sorry, I misjudged you too."

Terence said before leaving. I was left feeling a wide array of emotions in that moment, but mostly I finally felt at peace with Jennifer's death. Crystal may have died a horrible death but I'm sure Jenifer was up in heaven looking down at us, smiling.

Chapter Ten

After I had completed my task of viewing the flat, I headed off to Rosie's Café. I was ready for my meeting with Gabriela, I'd packed my uniform in my bag just in case the meeting ran longer than expected. There was no way I would get in the door wearing it, Rosie and Crosby had been at odds for over ten years, ever since she had opened up not far from him. She offered service with a smile alongside pretty decent food, as opposed to questionable slop and a side order of stomach cramps.

He had reduced his prices just to keep his dwindling clientele from leaving, the people came for the price but most definitely not for the service; or the food for that matter. I had never personally been into Rosie's

Cafe but I had overheard many a conversation about her delectable waffles, I certainly couldn't afford much on her menu but I was willing to buy a coffee just to see if it was indeed that much better than Crosby's.

I felt nervous upon entering this fine establishment, it was clean enough to happily eat off of the floor; not that you would have wanted to with such inviting seats. There were mahogany leather booths with cream tables on the outskirts of the Cafe, whereas mahogany tables alongside cream leather chairs were featured in the centre; it was pleasing to the eye whilst smelling delicious.

The food aromas filled my nostrils as I entered into the hum of happy customers chatting about the events of the day, nerves left me as it now felt as if life was going to be just fine whilst in the presence of such satisfied people. No one was shouting or complaining, the staff seemed to genuinely be happy to help with any of their needs or desires.

A lady standing by a podium greeted me cheerfully.

"Welcome to Rosie's Café, how can I help you today?"

She asked. Her name tag read 'Danielle'.

"I'm meeting someone by the name of Gabriela, is she here already?"

I asked. Danielle smiled.

"She's waiting for you at table seven, follow me please."

She led me to the table where she was sitting.

Gabriela seemed to glow as she sat there in the luminous lighting of the welcoming Cafe, I had only ever seen her in the grim, dull diner that I had the displeasure of working at. She was sat there as usual, reading her book while nursing a hot cup of java, as I made my way to join her at the table she spotted me.

"Anika, what a pleasure to see you out of work uniform."

Gabriela exclaimed in delight. She stood up, placing her book down as she leant in to kiss me on the cheek, I jumped in surprise, I wasn't used to such a friendly response from another human.

"Oh, sorry, I didn't mean to startle you... I was just saying hello."

She said. Concern filled her eyes.

"No, it's okay it was just unexpected, this is all new to me."

I replied. Gabriela and I sat down as she scrutinised me with her questioning eyes.

"So Anika, tell me a bit about yourself."

Gabriela asked. I shifted in my seat for a minute before relaxing, the waitress brought me a coffee which I could only presume was ordered for me by Gabriela.

"You can call me Anni if you like, there isn't much to tell, I have lived a pretty uneventful life."

I lied. Gabriela laughed joyously

© created by Scarlet Rivers 31st January 2018

"Well *Anni*, if I can be certain of anything it would be that your life most definitely *can't* have been 'uneventful'. You just ooze mystery from every crevice, plus you have a slight accent I can't place."

She said. I wasn't sure why she was so interested in my life, I was not about to divulge any information to a lady I had met merely twice in passing.

I just shrugged while laughing off her statement.

"If we are getting friendly enough for nicknames than you are welcome to call me Gabby. I am a nurse as you know, but I am also a stakeholder in Rosie's Café."

She revealed. I was surprised and it showed.

"So why come to Crosby's?"

I asked, feeling pensive.

"Firstly I came to check out the competition, however I returned the second time because of you Anni."

Gabriela said. It was my turn to scrutinise her as I stared at her intensely.

"What could you possibly want with me?"

I asked. Gabriela's smile was a little unnerving.

She seemed to have all the answers while revealing none.

"You impressed me, you looked as if you didn't belong in that cruddy place alongside the fact that you are a very good waitress."

I had originally thought that I would be discussing a nursing course when I now discover that I was being head hunted to potentially waitress elsewhere

"I don't understand, I thought we were here to discuss nursing."

Gabriela sipped her coffee before returning it back to its resting place

"Yes, well, no offence Anni but your a little old to get into the game of nursing. I do think you are far more capable than the job you are currently in allows you to show, the nursing thing was a ruse to get you here. I wanted you to see Rosie's Cafe firsthand before I offered you a job."

Gabriela revealed, causing me to feel a little deflated. I didn't know whether to be offended or feel flattered.

I sat there digesting the information she was feeding me.

"Okay… but, I can't give you a reference so I doubt you will want to employ me."

I said, Gabriela laughed at me in response

"Anni, I am your reference, I saw you at work and I have been raving about you to Rosie. She is short a waitress so has decided to employ you so long as you want the job."

She said. I looked around at the Café one more time, soaking it all in, I couldn't believe I could be working *here*

"It is just a starting place Anni, you could be trained in all areas of the business. Besides you can't say you'd rather be working for that old grouch Crosby."

She added. Gabriela seemed so enthusiastic about me working there, if only she knew my past and who I once was before now; would she still want to employ me then?

"Why would you vouch for me Gabby? I am a stranger to you, you don't know me very well. I didn't even finish school, so I have no documentation to offer you; I've never even applied for any ID."

I asked. I was feeling uneasy, this place was a little too nice for the likes of me.

"Look, I don't need to know the 'ins' and 'outs' of your life story. You seem to hold a world full of secrets in that head of yours but I trust that you will put your full effort into the job, and that is all that I need to know; for now. As for ID and qualifications, well leave that problem with me."

Gabriela said. I still didn't have much to say on the matter, I was just concerned about being surrounded by people so unlike me.

I looked down at my tummy then back up at an eager Gabriela.

"What about my baby? Surely that will be a big problem, no?"

I asked. Gabriela looked stern.

"Anni, that doesn't change a thing. We have plenty of girls who go on maternity leave, so long as you come back after the baby is born. Can you honestly say that Crosby won't fire you the second you start showing? That man has absolutely no loyalty, with us you will be fully trained in every department, paid handsomely and you'll receive paid time off while you have the baby. I'm kind of offering the deal of a lifetime here, so what's the hold up?"

She asked, she sounded slightly irritated. Gabriela seemed as though she wasn't going to take no for an answer.

"What shall I do about Crosby?"

I asked and as I did, Gabriela's smile returned.

"Leave Crosby to me."

She replied. Her smile seemed a little wicked as if she delighted in being the one to tell him he was going to lose his best waitress.

"How about I introduce you to Rosie and we get you a uniform? You *can* start now, right?"

She asked. With little other options available to me, I nodded in agreement as she guided me over to meet the owner of Rosie's Cafe.

Chapter Eleven

Rosie was like the anti-Crosby, she was slim alongside the fact that she actually looked clean, her demeanor was one of an experienced business woman. Her curt smile was off-putting as well as her elusive words, I watched her as she swayed from table to table until she reached our location.

"So this is the girl you told me about, she doesn't look like much."

Rosie said. I could tell straight away that she wasn't keen on hiring me.

"You haven't seen her in action yet, just trust me."

Gabriela said, she gave her a sincere look before encouraging me to speak.

"I… um…"

I started saying, trying hard to speak yet nothing coherent would come out.

"What? Are you waiting for me to hold your hand? Get to work!"

Rosie said. I felt very confused as I headed to the kitchen to find who was in charge. I was keen to do some tasks so that I could begin to prove my worth.

"Go collect orders from the tables."

A man wearing an apron said, I had my marching orders as soon as I had entered the kitchen.

"Put this on."

A lady who was also wearing an apron said. I was attempting to leave the kitchen area, a uniform was thrown in my direction alongside a notepad and a pencil.

I rushed to find the staff bathroom in order to change my clothes and found the state of the bathroom far more appealing than at Crosby's. They had hand towels accompanied by hand soap and to top it all off there was fully stocked toilet paper. I didn't have time to enjoy the toilet, I was in a hurry to change, shoving my clothes into the bag that I had brought with me I exited the bathroom in 'Rosie's Cafe' attire.

"What shall I do with my bag?"

I asked the lady that had given me the uniform.

"I'll put it in the office for you."

She said. I thanked her before hurriedly heading to the tables to get the orders from Rosie's customers.

Gabriela was still deep in conversation with Rosie, probably about me, I took about five orders before returning to the kitchen only to be sent back out with food for the other tables. The time flew by, mostly due to the sheer volume of customers in the Café. I enjoyed taking orders from these customers far more than the ones at Crosby's.

This was largely due to the fact that they actually asked politely for food or beverages, rather than snarling at me whilst demanding service. I must have been hard at work for at least four hours before Rosie came up to me, telling me to go on a break. I was a little surprised because at my old job I would have gotten one break in the course of a twelve hour shift, if I was lucky.

I was even offered free food from Rosie's Cafe for my break, I of course requested the waffles I had heard so many good things about, they certainly didn't disappoint. The warm soothing pastry melted in my mouth accompanied by nice cool vanilla ice cream, fluffy whipped cream and to top it all off it was drizzled in a warm caramel sauce.

I had quite literally never tasted anything so delicious in my entire life, my taste buds had been sent to heaven, I savoured every mouthful until the last bite when I was interrupted by Gabriela's presence.

"Good choice, those waffles are my favourite. How is your first shift going so far?"

Gabriela asked, her voice had summoned me back to reality. I gulped the food down quickly as I gave her my full attention .

"I didn't mind it, I could happily work here. What does Rosie have to say on the matter?"

I asked. Gabriela sat down opposite me on the break room table.

"She puts up a tough front but she likes you, I'm sure of it. Besides, she won't tell you this but once I saved her life up at the hospital, so she owes me. That's how I ended up going into business with her, we are good friends now."

Gabriela confessed. I didn't quite understand why Gabriela was practically strong arming Rosie into letting me have a job at this Café, but I wasn't willing to question it either; working here is like a walk in the park compared to Crosby's Diner.

The rest of my shift went smoothly, Gabriela had disappeared before I was ready to go home so it was Rosie who said the final goodbye to me.

"Well done for today Anika, I can see why Gabriela was so enthusiastic about you. You put a hundred and ten percent into your work."

She said. I wasn't sure how to respond to her words, I ended up just shyly grinning while I think I said 'Thank You'. She eyed me up and down before saying anything further, I felt as if she had decided to be my judge and jury all in one.

"The job is yours, I expect you to work six days a week with alternating shift patterns of my choice. You will be allowed a certain amount of paid holiday alongside time off when the baby comes. I do not want your pregnancy to get in the way of your job nor do I want the baby to interfere with your return to work either. If you can be back to work within three months after the baby is born then the job will be kept for you. That is the best I can offer you."

She said. Rosie was extremely stern but I accepted all of her terms and conditions.

My pay rate was a dollar more than I'd been paid at Crosby's per hour, which was a bonus in itself let alone having better work conditions; that's without mentioning better customers to serve. I idolised Rosie, if she can come up out of nothing and make a name for herself in the business world, there was hope for me yet.

I wish I had made something of myself before it had all come to this, not that I really had a choice about how my life was going to turn out. I couldn't wait to get home in order to tell Bryan all about my day, he would be thrilled that I had a new job.

Chapter Twelve

It must have been close to midnight before I made it home, as I opened the door I overheard part of a conversation between Bryan and an unknown person on the other side of the phone.

"I know that already, you don't have to remind me!"

My fiancé said. Bryan's tone was severe as he spoke into the receiver.

"We will discuss this tomorrow."

He added, with those final words he hung up the phone.

I couldn't help but wonder if I was the reason for such an abrupt end to the conversation.

"Hey Anni, how was work?"

Bryan asked, his voice had returned back to his normal, cheerfully, happy tone.

"Great."

I replied, Bryan kissed me on the cheek whilst looking awfully confused.

"I have never once heard you describe working with Crosby as 'great' before."

He said, I was unsure how to break the news to him, the odd conversation that I had just heard was a bit off-putting.

"I was offered another job today."

I revealed, before I could explain any further Bryan interrupted me.

"Well that was a bit silly of them, didn't they know you were pregnant?"

Bryan asked dismissively, he clearly wasn't in the best of moods but I tried my best to plod on.

"Rosie's Cafe, they know about the baby and they still want me to work there."

I said. With his brow furrowed alongside his lip downturned, I assumed he was impressed at the thought of my upgrade in the job department.

"I accepted, I have just come from a shift."

I added. Whilst saying that I removed my coat revealing my new uniform for him to glance at.

"Well the uniform looks good on you."

He said, I had gained his interest as he pulled me in towards where he was sitting, his tender kisses of course led to the usual sexual escapades. We never even made it off of the sofa.

I was always his, anywhere, anyplace, my whole body burned for his love all day long. After we had finished making love he finally remembered to ask me about the flat that he had begged me to see.

"How was the flat? Was it fit for a princess?"

He asked. I couldn't help but chuckle over his insinuation that I was a princess of all things.

"I liked it, you can see construction out of the window but that won't be forever. Other than that it was near perfect."

I said. He seemed pleased with my answer. I felt the need to inform him about my strange encounter today.

"Funny story about today, your realtor was Crystals old flame."

I said, trying to keep the conversation light.

"Did he say anything bad to you? I can make sure he never sees any commission from us."

He replied with a stern expression. I smiled at his need to protect me at all costs.

"No, it was fine. We both miss her, I think I helped him make peace with his loss a little bit. He definitely helped me come to terms with her passing."

I said. Bryan smiled.

"So you're okay?"

He asked. I nodded as he headed off to the shower, after a few minutes he shouted.

"Aren't you coming to join me beautiful?"

He asked, I laughed as I ran fully naked jumping in behind him.

We were there like two teenagers giggling as the water cascaded all over us. Since I became pregnant Bryan seemed more ravenous than ever, the second I placed my hands on his glistening brown skin his member stood to attention as if we didn't just have sex ten minutes prior to that moment.

My senses had all been heightened ever since falling pregnant, so orgasms were far easier to achieve and much more fulfilling than before. As we made love a second time in the shower I screamed out in ecstasy as he entered in and out of my body, his speed increased with every groan of delight I made.

We seemed to make love for hours, in reality it was probably more like twenty minutes; nevertheless I slept like a baby that night unlike Bryan. I had gotten up to wee, seeing as I did that a lot now I was with child, Bryan had not been in my bed, he was on the sofa just staring at the TV despite the fact that it was off.

I wasn't sure if I should bother him or not, he wasn't very forthcoming when talking about things that bothered him. I decided to be brave, I made my way into the lounge in order to sit next to him. He was so engrossed in the staring competition he had started with the television that he didn't even notice my presence, so much so in fact that he jumped when I gently brushed his arm with my palm.

"Anni, you scared me."

He revealed, I would normally leave him alone but I felt this needed to be questioned.

"What's going on Bryan? I heard that conversation earlier, you haven't been yourself all evening."

I asked. Bryan's sigh was loud and long.

"It's nothing to worry about Anni."

He replied. The disbelief adorned on my face led him to pause before revealing what it was that was really going on. A truth which shocked me to my core.

Chapter Thirteen

Bryan had always been a strong, quiet man. He often walked around with the weight of the world upon his shoulders, yet never once had chosen to let me in before now. I should have been happy that he was finally including me, although upon hearing what he had to say I suddenly wished I had never asked. I hadn't decided on how I should respond to this new information just yet.

"My office will be sending some pictures over for you to have a look at."

Bryan said in conclusion. I was in a spin of confusion.

"But, I don't have a sister."

I said defiantly. Bryan squeezed my hand, he had kept this information from me for weeks.

"Why didn't you tell me sooner?"

I asked, feeling defensive. Bryan looked like a hurt puppy dog, one who had just been scolded for peeing on the floor.

"I had to find out if there was any truth to it all."

He pleaded. I couldn't process what had just been said, I shook Bryan's hands off of mine.

"Explain to me again, from the beginning. Please."

I pleaded back. My shell had become hardened but Bryan understood, I knew this wasn't his fault.

I just had to hear it again, just to let it wash over me once more.

"Okay Anni, if you need to hear it again, here we go. While I was in prison I was attacked, when the man was beating me up he was also trying to get me to talk about your family. He was polish, I recognised some of his dialect. He was a large bald guy with this crowned eagle tattoo on the back of his head with the word 'polska' written below it, a tattoo which most definitely would have been considered racist. He kept asking about you, except he thought your name was Zofia Kowalski."

He said. Bryan kept checking my face to make sure I wasn't freaking out. I nodded so that he would continue.

"Once I was released I researched that name, the records were heavily sealed but I managed to get hold of adoption records for both you and your sister. You were younger than her, it is quite possible that you don't remember even

being adopted. Your sister's name was, at the time, Zuzanna Kowalski. The only reason I believed them even without the beating was because they described a birthmark which you have, they knew the location and everything. I have been unable to find anything else out about your family, everything before your adoption has been sealed. I also can't seem to find out any other information about what happened to your sister, but there was pictures from when you were adopted that had been kept on record. You can look at them tomorrow, see if it sparks any memories."

Bryan added finally. It didn't sound any better the second time around. How could I have a sister that I didn't know about, let alone have been adopted? My parents had been there since I could remember, they took me to school back in Poland.

They had pictures of me from a very young age, however I had never seen baby pictures of me. I had asked my parents about it once but they just said that they were poor when I was born, so much so that they couldn't afford even one picture of me.

"Even if this is true, which I'm struggling to believe right now, it doesn't change what I have been through to get here. This sister of mine

may not remember either, it isn't much to go on so far. My birthmark has been seen by way too many people to be definitive proof."

I reminded him, I had become cagey but Bryan couldn't let it lie.

"Even if there is a slim chance that this is all true... don't you want to know where you come from?"

He asked. I shrugged as I headed off back to bed. I was exhausted from the conversation, let alone the fact I had worked all day only to be woken up by all of this drama. Bryan climbed in behind me gripping me tightly, he gently stroked my stomach as he whispered in my ear.

"Should I have left things alone? Should I have kept it to myself? Come on Anni, talk to me."

He asked. I was quiet for what felt like five minutes while Bryan was nestled into the back of my neck.

"No, if it's true, I want to know. It is just a lot."

I replied. He had been drifting slowly off to sleep before I startled him with my whispers, he jolted slightly when I had begun speaking.

He hugged me in tighter, it was as if a weight had been lifted off of his shoulders. Unfortunately I was now the bearer of that burden, I drifted off to sleep questioning my very being. Who was I? I wrestled all night with strange dreams of things foreign to me, family is something I had lived without for far too long to even consider the idea that I may not even know who my family actually was.

I woke up feeling hot, sweat dropped off my face as I looked around the room. Somebody was calling my name, my birth name, the room had a red hue as the strange voice echoed around. I tried hard to find where the voice was coming from to no avail, I shouted into the abyss of nothingness asking who they were and to show themselves. A dark figure came to me from behind the curtains, the sinisterly dark face was unrecognisable to me.

As it came closer I jolted awake, I puffed and panted as I looked around the room which was now back to a normal colour again. I saw Bryan still fast asleep besides me, phew, it was just a bad dream. I felt warm and unsettled so I decided to run a bath, I had to be up soon anyway. I ran the bath to a nice warm temperature and just sat in the bath water filled with bubbles. Once in the tub I felt the water surround me and I dove my head backwards into the water, first making sure my eyes and nose were fully closed.

I held myself there for a manner of seconds before raising my face out of the water, I then rested the back of my head against the edge of the bath. With my eyes still closed I used my foot to turn on the hot tap little by little, just long enough to make the once warm water now blazing hot.

Sometimes when I was feeling down about life I liked to feel something other than what the world made me feel inside, the burning water helped me to forget all of the worries and stresses whilst also relaxing my aching muscles. Bryan didn't like me doing it as he was scared for the safety of my skin, but with a night like I just had to endure I needed it.

He caught me just as I was leaving the bath, the steam lifted from my body which now had a red colouring to it. Only slight but noticeable nevertheless, it would settle down back to normal after a few minutes out of the water. Unfortunately for me Bryan noticed it instantly.

"Anni, I have told you before, it's not good for you. What about the baby?"

Bryan exclaimed. I had nearly forgotten that I was pregnant with all the stress of last night, I do hope this wouldn't cause a problem.

© created by Scarlet Rivers 31st January 2018

"I'm sorry, I didn't even consider it would be a problem."

I replied sheepishly. I laid down on the bed still covered in just a towel, as I stayed still I hoped to feel the baby make some movement inside of me. Bryan sat next to me placing his hand on my stomach, just then the baby kicked exactly where Bryan's hand was.

It was subtle but he felt it all the same.

"WOW! Was that the baby?"

He asked excitedly. I nodded as he lay his head close to his hand, his grin was a beautiful sight as he lay there on top of me.

"We made that."

I stated as he looked up at me, then back to the small bump which was now showing. I felt so blessed to have my two favourite humans so close to me, I hoped desperately for a boy, I wouldn't wish my life on a child.

Men seem to get more chances, more opportunities in this life; compared to women. I only wanted the one child, I secretly prayed every morning for a little boy. Whether it was being answered or not I wouldn't know until the day of my baby's birth, a day which seemed to get farther away instead of closer.

Bryan kissed me briefly before we both got up, in order to get dressed and ready for work; he wanted to get in early to get the pictures for me. I was dreading seeing those old photos, as much as I was keen also to see what they showed. I just had to get work over and done with first.

Chapter Fourteen

I was slightly concerned still, about the baby; because of the bath incident. My doctors appointment was at the end of this week coming up, so it would give me a chance to discuss what had happened with the midwife. For now my main concern was getting to work on time, I was able to get dressed and out of the house on time but the bus hadn't arrived yet. I really didn't want to be late for my first real shift.

I was about to call a taxi when a car pulled up next to me, as the window started to come down I could see that Gabriela was the one inside of it.

"Jump in!"

Gabriela said as she swung the door wide open, so that I could sit in beside her.

"Why do you look so surprised?"

She asked. I was a little thrown by the fact that she not only seemed to know where I was, but also knew that I needed a lift. I didn't really believe in coincidences.

"It's just… how did you know that I was going to be here?"

I asked. Gabriela laughed outrageously at my suspicion.

"I pass this way to work all of the time, I just happened to see you while I was driving past. I assumed you wanted a lift considering all of the angry people at the bus stop, unless you would prefer to wait with them."

She replied innocently. I potentially was just over reacting, it had been a long night.

"Oh, sorry, I was just about to call a cab actually."

I revealed. Gabriela continued driving while still finding me incredibly hilarious.

"Well it looks like I came just in the nick of time, I'll drop you off to Rosie's on my way to the hospital."

She replied. I found it very hard to trust people's intentions towards me, but can you blame me? Considering the fact that anyone who had ever been nice to me, had always had an ulterior motive.

"Are you alright Anni? You seem a little off today."

Gabriela asked. My mind was elsewhere, I jolted back to reality when her words finally reached me as we pulled up in the Cafe's parking lot.

"I'm okay."

I replied. Gabriela looked at me in disbelief.

"Hurry up and get in before you're late."

She exclaimed. I smiled as I exited the vehicle, I briefly thanked her before reaching the service entrance of the Cafe.

As I arrived inside of Rosie's Cafe I was greeted by the smell of delicious bacon on the grill alongside eggs Being fried, it certainly beat the gruesome smell of Crosby's odorous unwashed body that was for certain.

"Welcome back Anika, you have customers waiting to be served."

Rosie's said, her way of greeting me surpassed Crosby's, considering she hadn't berated me within the first five minutes of my shift. I hurried out to take orders, I hadn't even noticed the face of the person who I was actually taking orders from.

"So this is where you ran off to then."

Was said. It was Crosby, I couldn't recognise him out of his filthy uniform, he had actually washed before coming here.

I just stared, I was at a loss for words.

"Good riddance, didn't need your crappy excuse for work anyway. Now go get my coffee."

He snarked. It took me a minute to regain my composure.

"Certainly, Sir."

I said as I did a weird sort of half curtsy before sheepishly heading back to the kitchen.

Rosie had already made the coffee for him, so when I got there she turned me back around with the coffee now in my hands. She frog marched me back to his table, I felt as though I was in between two divorced parents not knowing what to say.

"Here you go Crosby, I do hope you aren't harassing my staff."

Rosie said, he took the coffee and had a sip before placing it back on the table.

"You mean *my* ex member of staff, no I wouldn't dream of it Rosie."

Crosby sneered. Rosie ushered me to leave so that is exactly what I did, I tended to the other tables whilst she carried on talking with Crosby. I couldn't catch the whole conversation but the bits I did hear weren't good.

Crosby insinuated that Rosie stole me from him leaving his diner short staffed, he also went on to demand compensation for his loss of earnings due to having no staff to cover my shifts. Rosie mocked him by offering him ten dollars saying that it can't be more than that amount of money that he lost in takings, she seemed to be far from threatened by the oaf.

After winning the argument she went back into her office, Crosby decided to leave quietly after he had finished his drink. In amongst all of the happily chatting customers the conversation had been barely noticeable, to all but me of course. I was surprised to see Rosie stick up for me, seeing as she seemed to have not wanted to employ me in the first place. Perhaps she had now seen my worth since joining her staff. Aside from that one incident, my second shift at Rosie's Cafe went off without a hitch.

Chapter Fifteen

Customers tips were divided up between all of the waitresses, I was handed a wad of cash at the end of the day as my part of the tips. I tried returning it which made the other girl laugh.

"You worked hard girl, and you're pregnant. Time to enjoy the rewards! We got your tips yesterday seeing as you were on a trial shift, now you're one of us."

The girl talking was called Sandy, she loved chewing gum along with wearing hair in pigtails. She had to have been about nineteen, her hair shone like the sun with glossy strawberry blonde strands bunched up together.

She winked at me as I pocketed the cash whilst thanking them. I half expected them to be mean or jealous due to the fact I was taking some of their tips, however it was the complete opposite. I think I was going to like working here, I still felt like I didn't belong but that was fading slowly.

Rosie proudly gave me a copy of the new rota that she had now finished, I thanked her as I looked at my name written clear as day in black and white. There was a certain thrill to being an official employee, I never thought I would enjoy the normality as much as I truly did. The simple things in life that others took for granted gave me such joy inside, my name was planted all over that rota.

Just as I was leaving work Gabriela showed up again, she was there in her car waiting in the carpark. I was certain she had upgraded to stalker overnight, was she there for *me*? I walked straight past her car in order to go for the late bus, I needed to get home so that I could look at the pictures Bryan had acquired for me.

"Anni, hold up."

Gabriela shouted. I acted surprised to see her so as not to alert her to my concern.

"Oh, hi. I didn't see you there."

I had to lie, she got me this job, I couldn't risk losing it now.

"Jump in, I'll drop you home."

She offered. Did she somehow know where I lived too? I got in the car feeling wary of the company I was now keeping.

"So, tell me everything. How was your day?"

Gabriela asked. She seemed so eager to know how I was doing in my new job; it was bewildering to say the least.

"Good, thanks."

© created by Scarlet Rivers 31st January 2018

I said, my response seemed not to be what she had wanted to hear.

"Come on Anni, Rosie told me that your old Boss came to harass you."

Gabriela revealed. This must have been what she wanted to talk about, perhaps that was why she had come to pick me up.

"Yeah, he did. Rosie spoke to him for me."

I answered. Gabriela looked at me fairly intensely, this unnerved me and not just because her eyes weren't where they should be when driving.

"You don't talk much, do you Anika?"

She said, finally. Her eyes were now back on the road at least, what was it that this woman wanted from me?

"I have never needed to before."

I said quietly whilst staring out of the window, Gabriela was pulling up outside of my flat.

"How did you know my address?"

I asked feeling nervous. Gabriela laughed at me.

"It's in your employment record Anni."

She replied. I hadn't thought about that, perhaps paranoia had just became a part of who I was by this stage in my life.

I thanked her for the lift as I tried to exit the vehicle.

"You're not going to invite me in?"

She asked. I froze as she raised one eyebrow, I could tell what was happening here. It wasn't the first female to show interest in me.

"I have a fiancé, I am not interested in woman, in *that* way. Is that okay?"

I asked. Gabriela just looked at me in disbelief.

"I'm sorry, what? You think I'm gay? Anni have you never had anyone try to be nice to you before?"

She asked. I thought long and hard about the question she had presented me with.

Truthfully I'd only had people pay this much attention to me when they had wanted something from me.

"Well, no, actually."

I replied honestly. The expression on her face had transformed from horror into sympathy in a manner of seconds.

"What kind of life have you led?"

She queried. I wasn't willing to answer that question incase it led to me losing my job, so I just smiled awkwardly in reply.

"Would you like to come in?"

I asked after an awkward silence. This made her giggle return.

"I gotta run but another time, okay?"

She said. I think she sensed my awkwardness over the situation and let me off, thankfully, I raced upstairs without looking back in case she changed her mind again.

Bryan was waiting for me in front of our tiny box TV, there was an ominous looking file on top of the coffee table in front of him. I fell into the chair next to him, I couldn't wait to get off of my feet. Bryan grabbed my feet and placed them in his lap, after removing my shoes he started to gently rub my feet.

"Hard day at work?"

He asked. I couldn't even get words out so I just nodded before getting a kiss planted on my lips.

"How was *your* day?"

I asked in return . His kiss must have brought some life back into me because my words had come back to me, as I was able to reply finally.

"Productive."

He picked up the sealed envelope while grinning at me, then placed it in my hands.

"You didn't open it?"

I asked. Bryan shook his head.

"This is for you."

Bryan replied, he was such a gem, always selfless while trying hard to care for me. The contents of the envelope was not at all what I was expecting.

Chapter Sixteen

Bryan just looked at me expectantly, as I peered into the large brown envelope. I had expected photos of my family, but instead I just got one solitary picture of what I had to assume was my sister and I.

"Is this it?"

I asked as I pulled out the lonely picture in order to let Bryan see it.

"That's weird, the lady on the phone said there were pictures, plural."

Bryan revealed, the envelope seemed oversized for just one picture. I tipped it upside down just to see if there were any other items inside.

As I shook the envelope a rolled up piece of paper fell out, which had a rubber band wrapped around it. I took off the rubber band in order to read the message, when a key suddenly fell out of the rolled up paper. The note read as follows:

This key will lead you to the answers you seek.

That was it, I find out my parents weren't my parents and that I have a sister I never even knew, now I have a cryptic note alongside a key and I have no idea what it opens.

Bryan tried to ring the lady back, in order to question her about the solitary photo, however the number had been disconnected. Somebody, somewhere did not want me to know who I was, or where I came from. I looked at the photo again, on the back of the photo was some writing; it said **'Zofia age one left'** and **'Zuzanna age six right'** but it was written in polish. In the adoption records that were faxed over to Bryan it said that I was adopted at the age of just four, which would mean my sister would have been nine at the time.

I had no clue as to where she was now, or if she was even still alive.

"It's okay, Anni, we will get to the bottom of this."

Bryan said, trying to reassure me. I agreed with him but I was concerned as to what problems would ensue, if we continued trying to get to the bottom of who I really was.

"What do you think this key opens?"

I asked, knowing full well he wouldn't have any more of a clue than I did. He examined the key closely but came up empty all the same.

"I honestly don't know, perhaps a storage locker or even a safety deposit box."

Bryan said, offering very little help.

I placed the key on a neck chain that I happened to be wearing before placing it back around my neck.

"I'll just have to wear it until we figure it out."

I said as I began unbuttoning my uniform. Bryan began looking at me longingly, I knew exactly what he wanted, I was exhausted from work but who could say no to that hunk of a man. He had become insatiable ever since my baby bump had started to show. Something about me carrying his child really got his juices going.

He carried me into the bedroom, as we began to make love I couldn't help but think about the situation I was in. My whole body quivered in excitement as he licked my nipples, images of my lost sister and mysterious notes faded as he entered inside of me. That was tomorrow's problem, for now I was going to enjoy being with the man that I loved. Judging by how engorged he had become as he fondled my enlarged breasts, he too was enjoying himself.

After our quick but satisfying romp under the covers, I fell straight to sleep. The next morning I actually slept in for once, I was on a late shift which meant Bryan was the first one out the door today. It was going to be a busy week, I had my doctor's appointment tomorrow then we were moving to the new place on the weekend.

I was working Saturday, but off on the Sunday so I had made a deal with Bryan; he would pack up our stuff and move them to the new house and I would unpack everything the next day. I definitely wasn't sad to say goodbye to this crummy apartment, the only good memories I had were since Bryan had come out of prison. In fact since the day my parents died, Bryan had been the only good thing to remember.

I was rudely awoken by the buzzing of my intercom, somebody was calling through to my flat number. I was going to ignore it so that I could try and go back to sleep, however I considered that it could have been Bryan saying that he had forgotten his keys or something. I figured I was better off at least finding out who it was and what they wanted.

Of all the people it could have been, I had not expected to hear Gabriela's voice booming through.

"Hey Anni, it's me, Gabby. Let me in."

Her shrill voice torpedoed my eardrums. Did this woman never give up?

Chapter Seventeen

I wondered if I should pretend I wasn't in, but where would that lie lead me? Nowhere good I susie t. I buzzed her up then raced to get some clothes on. She was there knocking on my door just as I got my last item of clothing on.

"What brings you here at this time of the morning?"

I asked. Gabriela looked at her watch then back to me.

"Sorry to break it to you, it is twelve already."

She revealed. I really *had* slept in late, thank goodness I didn't start work until two in the afternoon.

"Okay, so what brings you here at this time of day?"

I said, changing my question accordingly. Gabriela held out a cup of coffee and a pastry.

"For you, I thought I would take you up on the offer to come in."

She said. Did she mean the offer that I extended her way the previous night, while under duress?

"Thanks?"

I said hesitantly before taking the coffee and pastry off of her hands, then sat on my sofa.

"You can join me if you like."

I offered. She didn't need telling twice, Gabriela immediately sat down besides me.

"Don't you have anything better to do today?"

I asked, not meaning for it to come out how it sounded, thankfully she didn't take offense.

"Not today, no."

She replied. I had noticed that the picture and envelope were still on my coffee table so I quickly placed the coffee and pastry on top of them so that she wouldn't see them.

I wasn't sure why I was so eager to hide them, I guess I just didn't like people knowing things about me.

**"Are you going to drink that? It's decaffeinated
if that's what you're worrying about."**

Gabriela said, I started drinking the still warm cup of coffee in order to not arouse suspicion.

"Delicious, thanks."

I said with a forced smile. She grinned as she watched me, there was something very strange about her interest in me. If she wasn't gay, then why was she so keen to be involved in my life.

Perhaps she was an undercover cop, or working for ICE.

**"So, Gabby, tell me about yourself. I really don't
know much about you."**

I said, trying my best to inconspicuously gather intel. Gabriela shuffled in her seat slightly.

**"Not much to tell really, what did you want to
know?"**

I thought for a minute.

"Do you have any sisters or brothers? How did you become a nurse? Are you married? Things like that I guess."

I said, realising I wasn't quite as subtle as I intended initially. Gabriela laughed joyously.

"Well, no I am single and I am also an only child. I became a nurse when I was twenty, I am twenty-five now and my favourite colour is blue. Is that enough about me yet?"

Gabriela asked. She did not look twenty-five, if anything she looked older than me. If I had to guess she would be at least five years older.

"Your turn, tell me about you Anni."

She said, playing me at my own game. I looked at her face, I don't suppose she had any reason to lie to me so I just went with it.

"I am engaged to a black man, having his baby. Only child as well, however my parents aren't alive anymore."

I said, wanting to see her reaction to what I was saying but she seemed to not react at all.

"Tell me something I don't know."

She said in jest. I thought I just had, how much did this girl actually know about me.

"So you knew my parents were dead, how?"

I asked. Gabriela just shrugged.

"Didn't you say that already?"

She asked. I just shook my head looking at her intently.

"Oh, well you must just give off a 'dead parents' vibe then."

She replied without even blinking. I decided to try and get rid of her.

"Well this has been lovely, truly, I have to go and get ready for work now so shall I see you later?"

I asked, hoping her answer would be no. I started getting up in order to say goodbye, however Gabriela had other plans.

"Don't worry I can drop you to work on the way to the hospital."

She said. This woman was never going to leave me alone, that much was clear. I faked a happy smile.

"Okay, well I will have to jump in the shower. Are you going to wait here?"

I asked.

"I'm flattered Anni, but you see I'm not interested in women, in *that* way… you understand, right?"

Gabriela said, clearly teasing me. She chuckled happily before turning on the TV, while she was distracted I grabbed the photo so that I could take it to my bedroom.

I hid it in my room then got into the shower, I took a long time in the bathroom just to waste some more time away from her. She unsettled me, I had never had any female even acknowledge me before let alone have one try so eagerly to befriend me. Once I was ready and dressed in my room I headed back out to where she was still just happily watching TV.

I sat down besides her before eating the pastry she had brought for me, it was delicious, it reminded me so much of home in a way I couldn't explain.

"What is this?"

I asked, mesmerised by the flavours and light texture.
Gabriela turned off the TV before answering me.

"They call it 'Chruściki', or Angel Wings. It is from my local Polish shop."

Gabriela replied. I would normally be on high alert after hearing she was hanging out in polish shops, but I was on too much of a pleasure high from the food I was eating.

As I swallowed the last piece of the light and fluffy fried pastry I licked what I assumed was powdered sugar from my lips, I didn't really know how to respond to that.

"Maybe I can take you there one day."

Gabriela offered. I still had no response. I just got up to place the rubbish in the bin, making sure to take note of the shops' name.

"Shall we go now?"

She asked. For now I was going to remain quiet, I wasn't willing to reveal all of my cards just yet.

"I'm ready if you are."

I stated before opening my front door.

"Perhaps we could go to that Polish shop on the way to work?"

I asked. Gabriela was taken aback a little.

"It is a bit far away for that, another day."

She said. I thought she passed by my house in order to get to work, so how far did she live from me if it was too far away to go to right now? We had plenty of time before I started for a detour, the coffee was still warm so it couldn't be that far from here.

Things weren't adding up, this woman had secrets and I was determined to find out what they were.

"Okay, next time."

I said before getting into her car, without making a sound for the entire journey. I knew of a Polish shop not too far from Rosie's Cafe. My plan was to go to that shop and speak with its owner when I was allowed to go for my break. I could see if they knew of this other polish place or not.

Chapter Eighteen

The lady in the Polish shop was very friendly, I spoke to her in my own language to ask about the pastry that Gabriela had given me. I asked her if I could buy some or even if there was a place that I could get a hold of some easily. She told me that there was only one place in town that sold them, they were time consuming and difficult to make which is why they weren't easy to get a hold of.

She told me that in our culture they were usually only made for special occasions and weddings, so how was it that Gabriela had one this morning to share with me. If you have to pre order them in advance there was no way that she could have just picked one up along the way to my house, I thanked the store owner before leaving to get back to work. The strangest thing was the name on the pastry packet, it had apparently gone out of business weeks ago.

I arrived just in time to eat some food before returning back to work. Unfortunately this meant I didn't get to sit down for very long, my feet would have to pay the price for my curiosity. I half expected Gabriela to rock up outside of the Cafe after my shift again but this time she didn't, I was relieved that she hadn't been there but it only made my distrust of her intentions grow.

There were a few things that I was sure of, Gabriela knew more about me than she was letting on, she was potentially a threat to me alongside the fact that she was lying directly to my face. I had no idea who she really was or what she actually wanted from me. Armed with proof of her dishonesty, I was going to confront her about it, but I didn't see her for over a month.

I had other things to distract me going on, the doctor's appointment went well, the baby is still happy, healthy and kicking. I was becoming certain that I was pregnant with a boy as the baby loved to kick me, as if there was some sort of ball in there with it. My tummy had grown larger now, but still could be hidden with large clothing items such as coats and jumpers.

I was now twenty-four weeks pregnant, Bryan and I had settled down nicely into our new apartment, he had even gone as far as to set up a nursery for the baby. I had just come home from a long shift at Rosie's Cafe when Bryan greeted me with an unusually suspicious looking smile.

"How was your day?"

He queried. I looked at him knowing that he was up to no good.

"Good, what are you up to?"

I asked. Bryan laughed at me.

"You can always figure me out, I have a surprise for you."

Bryan said right before he grabbed our coats, then we headed down to the car together.

"Where are we going?"

I asked. Bryan kissed me briefly.

"It's a surprise."

He revealed. We drove for a short time before arriving at a church, weirdly it was a roman catholic church which largely consisted of a Polish congregation. This was probably because there were a lot of Polish people living in the surrounding area.

"Why are we here?"

I asked. Bryan grinned from ear to ear.

"I have finally convinced the Minister to marry us, with the help of a large donation to their church alongside a sob story about your life. Well, parts of it."

He revealed. I was in awe of how amazing my soon to be husband was. He'd gone to so much trouble just to be officially married to me.

The minister had agreed to the service so long as it was a private affair. Not many churches would be willing to marry a black man to a white woman, let alone make it public knowledge.

"You did this all for me?"

I asked, feeling teary. Bryan pulled me into face him.

"I would do anything for you Anni."

He admitted. We kissed before entering the church, I whispered to Bryan as we crossed the threshold.

"Are we really going to get married in these clothes?"

I asked quietly. He laughed softly.

"Of course not, our change of clothes are waiting for us."

Bryan revealed as he guided me to a changing area that had been set up for me, he went off to change into his suit while I dared to open the dress that he had bought for me.

It was a very simple elegant white gown, nice and flowy so that it would drape over my baby bump while covering it nicely. A lady was there to help me get dressed then she applied some makeup, I looked like a princess. I held the flowers in my hand before I got ready to walk down the aisle, the room was completely empty aside from a few leaders of the church.

The organ began to play as I walked down to stand besides Bryan, he looked so handsome and distinguished in his smart suit. He wore a lovely grey suit with a white shirt, to complete it all off nicely he wore black shoes and a matching tie. I had never seen him look happier than in that moment as he saw me dressed in white, standing before him.

He mouthed the word **'WOW'** as he gazed upon me, the Minister ran through all of the marriage vows without so much as a pause. We repeated the bits we were suppose to, rings were exchanged then we were allowed to kiss. We were now officially man and wife, it was without a doubt the best moment in my entire life.

After the paperwork was all signed Bryan swept me off my feet as he placed me inside of the back seat in the car, we drove to our apartment shortly after the ceremony. Every part of that night was perfect, we made love like never before, I was overcome with such emotion that I only knew how to express one way.

I went into work the next day with the new ring upon my finger, without saying a word to anyone they all knew something was different. I was happy for once, they didn't often see me smile but when they saw the ring the girls got excited and congratulated me. I was on a complete high until I reached one of the booth's where Gabriela happened to be sitting in.

"Hi, Gabby, long time no see. Are you okay?"

I asked. Gabriela looked up at me.

"I hear congratulations are in order."

Gabriela stated. She didn't even smile.

"Coffee please Anika."

She said plainly. I had wanted to see what was wrong, however the café was busy so I just got on with my job. She didn't even acknowledge my existence when I handed her the hot beverage.

"Did I do something wrong to you?"

Was said abruptly. I heard Gabriela's voice cut through the mindless chatter of content customers as I cleared away some dirty dishes.

"No, why?"

I replied. Gabriela had stood up and began walking over to me.

"So why no invite to the wedding? I thought we were friends."

Gabriela pouted. So this was why I had received the cold shoulder treatment.

"Nobody got an invite, it was a surprise wedding with only members of the clergy to witness it."

I said. Gabriela nodded briefly before leaving Rosie's establishment.

"Anika I need to see you for a moment."

Rosie was summoning me into her office, I couldn't help but wonder if my worst fears were about to be realised.

Chapter Nineteen

I had a feeling of impending doom lurking inside, with Gabriela upset I somehow feared I'd be soon out on my arse. I went into her office very quietly with my head as low as the ground.

"Chin up Anika, it isn't anything bad."

Rosie said, as though she were reading my mind. I barely contained my relief as I sat in the opposing chair to hers.

"I just need to know when you are going to be off, in order to have the sprog. I assume your midwife has given you the required information by now."

She added. I hadn't even considered when I would leave work.

The baby was growing inside of me, but so far not much had changed in my life. I hadn't thought about what would happen when it had actually arrived.

"Oh, um… well."

I said, stumbling for a reply.

"Spit it out girl."

Rosie said impatiently.

"I'm due in January so I was going to work into the first week of the new year."

I said, finally. Rosie seemed satisfied with that and shooed me out of her office. As I was getting ready to leave she spoke again.

"I didn't take you for someone brave."

She said. I turned back around to face her looking confused.

"Brave?"

I queried. She tilted her head slightly.

"Marrying someone out of your race, you either have to be brave or mad... right?"

She said. I blushed a little.

"Is it going to be a problem?"

I asked softly. Rosie looked at me without showing any emotion.

"He who casts the first stone and all that."

She replied dismissively. I was sure that was her way to insinuate that my love for Bryan was somehow a sin, if only she knew what sin truly stained me. Her attention was now firmly on her desk so I decided to take my leave. I wasn't sure how to feel about that conversation but I suppose it could have gone worse.

I worked hard all day; the thought of my recently acquired husband waiting for me in our new flat kept me going. I couldn't wait to get home, Rosie's cafe was still busy as ever, increasingly so lately. I dread to think what the Christmas season would be like in this place. My experience of Christmas in Crosby's diner wasn't that impressive, it was just like any other day in the diner aside from a few festive decorations dotted about.

Bryan was snoring like a baby when I got home, by the time I finally crawled through the door and into my bed it was into the early hours of the morning. It seemed a shame to wake him so I gently kissed his cheek before drifting fast asleep beside him, but not before I had a good long think. It had been a tiresome day, from start to finish. I couldn't help but think on Gabriela's cold attitude towards me. She went from being all over me like a rash to avoiding me.

I considered whether I should try to mend fences, however I was just glad to have a break from the interest she had shown in me. I still found the incident with the angel wing dessert odd, I had wondered whether it had anything to do with my nickname when I worked for Ricardo. The more I mulled over it, the more I began to feel that I was just being paranoid.

Surely she never would have employed me knowing who I used to be. As I drifted off into a deep sleep, I slipped straight back into that strange dream I had after learning about my sister's existence. It happened exactly the same except this time, when the shadowy figure came closer, Gabriela had been the one calling me Zofia. I jolted awake, however thankfully I hadn't disturbed Bryan. Perhaps having Gabriela on my mind before sleeping had altered the dream.

As my husband lay next to me, still fast asleep, he looked so peaceful. I envied his ability to sleep so well undisturbed, I hadn't enjoyed a decent night sleep since my adoptive parents were murdered in front of me. That was so hard to digest, my adoptive parents, if only they were still alive so that I could find out the answers that I longed for. I got up so that I could splash my face with water, I couldn't face going back to sleep yet so I sat on my sofa instead.

I fiddled with the key that had arrived in the ominous envelope, I hadn't thought much about the envelope since Bryan had brought it home over a month ago now. We were no closer to finding out what this key opened, perhaps we were even further away now. I started thinking about that photo I had received. Perhaps if I looked at my sister's face again, it may spark some vague memory of a time now lost to me.

I went quietly into the bedroom to retrieve it, making sure not to disturb Bryan I came back into the lounge; holding onto it as if it were a lifeline. I opened the envelope in order to grab the photo of my sister and I, as hard as I searched it wasn't in there. I scraped around in the large brown envelope rather manically to try and find it but it had vanished.

As I shuffled my hand around I tore the envelope slightly, the tear was across the back which revealed a secret section inside the back of it. On first inspection the envelope looked like a normal brown posting device, once I had ripped the inner layer I found another couple of photos and a note. The note read as follows:

Dear Bryan, I am sorry I had to destroy the evidence which could have helped you get to the bottom of who Anika really is. Some lady came by demanding to have the files that I had found for you, I managed to save these two photos.

One is of Anika's adoptive parents and the other is of her sister, their names are written

at the back of each photo. I
hope this helps, the key is one
in a set of two. I believe it
opens a safety deposit box, you
need both keys to open it.

My belief is that Anika's
sister is in possession of the
other key, be careful because
this lady wasn't messing around.
I have disconnected my number
and will be laying low, if you
need to reach me call Mr
Hounslow.

That was it, true to her words there were two photos, the one of my sisters adoptive parents was on top.

I knew this instantly considering I didn't recognise them, they look very solemn as they stood there holding hands. The black and white old picture was a bit grainy however you could make out their faces just fine, the pair were the opposite to my adoptive parents. I placed the photos alongside each other, tears overwhelmed my eyes as I looked at my now dead adoptive parents.

They looked so innocent and unaware of their fate, how were they to know adopting me would lead to their untimely deaths. Images of their dead and bloody faces flashed before my eyes as I wept, I couldn't bare to look away from their loving faces. Bryan must have been startled by my sobs because he was waking up. I could hear rustling of sheets, I quickly stopped crying and dried my face.

"Is that you Anni? What happened? Why are you alone sobbing in the dark? What time is it?"

Bryan asked. Try as I might the words didn't come out of my mouth, so I just lifted up the picture that I had been holding tightly in my hands. Bryan rubbed sleep out of his eyes, he sat next to me before reading the note.

His face looked perplexed as he read through it a couple of times before piping up.

"Mr Hounslow? Whatever could she mean by that?"

He asked. I shrugged knowing far less than him about the full meaning behind the note.

"A code perhaps? At least we know the names of my sisters adoptive parents, that's a start right?"

I asked as I showed Bryan the back of the photo, Edwina and Henry Townsend, they were most definitely English names.

That wasn't the only strange thing about the whole matter, why were we separated in the first place? Let alone to two different countries, I was left in Poland and ended up in America so where did my sister end up? Was she still in England? I seriously doubt the English couple would have stayed in Poland with her, judging by their dress sense they had money.

They wore Victorian era clothing but were also adorned with accessories such as the pocket watch that Henry was sporting alongside the fancy broach Edwina had across the collar of her dress. Bryan mulled over the information he had been presented with.

"I can get my P.I. to investigate for us, it is a start yes. Not much of one though, I am just thinking about the clue Chrissy left for us in that note. Mr Hounslow, I saw a book in her office with that name on. Perhaps I should get my P.I. to look into that too."

Bryan revealed. He then turned his attentions back onto me.

"Can we go back to sleep now? How on earth did you discover this?"

He asked. I briefly explained to him how I had come across the information, then I followed him back to bed, this time having a nice dreamless sleep.

Chapter Twenty

The next day I woke up thinking about the missing photo, I started rummaging around the room for where it could have gotten to. My loud searching had caused Bryan to stir again, I didn't feel so bad this time seeing as he had to be awake in order to get ready for work.

"Did you put the picture of me and my sister somewhere?"

I asked, feeling anxious. Bryan looked at me clearly feeling a little confused.

"No Anni, I haven't seen it since the day it arrived. I assumed you kept it somewhere safe."

He replied.

"Well yes, I thought I had but it's not here."

I said in retaliation.

"Look don't worry so much, it can't have grown legs and walked away. It has to be here somewhere."

He said. I muttered under my breath saying, **'unless it was stolen.'** but he took no notice. After I had searched from top to bottom I knew it was nowhere, somehow it had been taken.

I replayed the day back through in my head; I had opened the envelope up, then looked at the contents before later being interrupted by Gabriela. I remembered hiding the envelope from her before putting it in my room, I hadn't thought to check if the photo was still in the envelope before we left the house. What if she took it while I was in the shower? I couldn't think of a reason why she would do such a thing, unless she saw it as an opportunity to find out who truly worked for her.

That would kind of explain the cold-shoulder treatment, except that the picture could have been of anyone, how was she to know it was me as a child? I thought about storming into work while demanding to speak with her, what if I was wrong? Who else could have taken it? Then I thought of her finding out who I use to be before working at Crosby's Diner, I didn't want to be fired, who knows if Crosby would even take me back now. Let alone the fact that I had taken a bite out of the good life, I certainly did not want to return back to the bad side of life.

I would keep quiet for now, it may still turn up in the house for all I knew. I got ready to go to Rosie's Cafe with a rather large bee in my bonnet about the missing photo, it was my only connection to a life I had never known that I was once a part of. Unfortunately there was no putting this genie back in its bottle, I knew now that I wasn't who I thought I was. I had to find out who Zofia really is, it felt strange thinking of myself as Zofia. I had been known by many names but never that one, I liked it but I had no connection to it; I couldn't see Bryan calling me Zofia all of a sudden.

Work went passed in a blur of customers yet again, I had been distracted by my own tormenting thoughts of the secrets that lay deep within my subconscious mind. I ran straight into a customer with a tray of napkins, the neatly folded material cloths that had been intended for the empty tables were now flying through the air. Unable to stop what I had accidentally set in motion I watched helplessly as each one landed in the most inappropriate places, while one fell into a cup of coffee the other landed on top of delicious hot waffles.

The others either fell on the floor or onto customers, I apologised to the man in front of me not recognising him at first.

"No worries, Angel."

He said. As the man winked at me memories of what felt like a past life came flooding back, he had been one of my regulars before I escaped Big Joe and his cronies. I saw him waltz passed me as if it were a normal event running into an ex hooker at the local Cafe, I started collecting my lost napkins while still staring intently so as to find out where he was headed.

He had walked into the back of the restaurant, the customers had been very understanding over the incident. I offered them new items off of the menu which of course would come out if my wages, the lady with the waffles declined my offer saying it was fine while the man with the coffee wanted a replacement.

I scooped up the others before heading to the back room in order to dump the dirty napkins, I grabbed another tray of them before heading back. I saw my ex client smooching a fellow waitress at Rosie's Cafe, I assume they were an item. I hustled off to grab the new coffee before placing the napkins where they were supposed to go in the first place.

I wasn't sure what to do about running into that guy, I think his name was Bill Sykes. I hadn't been in the game for so long now, for all I knew he didn't frequent Ricardo's club anymore, let alone the fact that they may not have been dating back when I was servicing him. I most certainly wasn't a friend of his girlfriend, Mindy wasn't very keen on new people from what I gathered.

Either way I wasn't about to 'out' myself just to tell her the history I shared with her boyfriend, I'd lose my job for starters let alone my dignity. I did feel bad for her but it wasn't my place to get involved, I was however, slightly concerned that she already knew about me or perhaps he was going to tell her now he had seen me working there. I managed to get through the rest of my shift without any other situations happening upon me, I was going to make it my mission to find out if Mindy knew anything about me.

I wasn't sure how I would do that yet, I could ask Gabriela to help me gain information from her had she still been my friend. I hadn't seen her for the whole shift, I did however spot her car waiting outside of the diner. I wasn't sure if she was there for me or not, I decided to go over to her car all the same.

"Hey Gabby, What brings you here?"

I asked. She opened the door, gesturing for me to get in the passenger seat beside her, I walked around to the open door before getting in.

"Are you okay? You seem off with me."

I queried. I half expected her to return to her joyous laughter at every other word that left my mouth, however cold silence was all that greeted me whilst sitting there patiently waiting for a reply. I received no such thing, however she did drive me home.

She pulled up outside of my apartment building and we sat in silence for what seemed an age.

"I had a sister once, she died, you remind me of her. I thought we shared a connection, when you didn't invite me to your wedding I felt offended. I apologise for over reacting."

Gabriela confessed. I wasn't sure how to respond to what she had just said. Part of me wanted to question her as to why she had lied about being an only child, although technically I had too, so I felt it was better not to open that can of worms.

"I have never had a friend before, I guess I just don't know how to act around you. I honestly didn't do anything intentional to offend you."

I said in reply. It wasn't much of a response but it was all that I had to offer.

"I forgive you."

Gabriela said, as she did her smile had returned, I hadn't remembered apologising but if it got her smile back then I guess I did something right.

I smiled back at her before trying to exit the car, I paused before turning back.

"Did you happen to see a photo laying around when you were in my house last?"

I asked. Gabriela shook her head.

"Not that I remember. Why? Was it of great importance to you? If you describe the photo maybe it will jog my memory."

She asked. There was something in her demeanour and tone of voice that led me to believe she wanted it to be important. Perhaps so that she could be helpful to me in some way.

"Oh, no, nothing important. I have just lost something that I was hoping to keep safe."

I said, I didn't want her knowing it's real value to me incase she was the one who took it. After closing the car door I left, without so much as looking back I went straight into the building. I was concerned to look back in case she figured me out. There was more to Gabriela than met the eye, I just wished I could figure it out without losing my job in the process.

Chapter Twenty-One

Bryan was awake when I entered my home this time, it was nice to see his handsome face especially after a day like today.

"Hey Anni."

He said. The way he spoke had me thinking that he had some unhappy news to give me.

"What is it? Did you find any new information?"

I asked. Bryan took a deep hard breath before continuing.

"My Private eye found out about the adoptive parents that took your sister in."

He said as he handed me a newspaper article, it was entitled **'Tragedy at the Townsend Mansion.'**.

It was a photocopy of a newspaper article that dated back nearly twenty-five years ago, it said that there was a blazing fire that had been deemed an accident by the local police. The place had gone up in flames, the whole family had been presumed dead. There were unidentifiable charred remains, judging by the article I was reading my sister had been turned into charcoal along with the Townsend Mansion. This didn't help anything, so what if the place went up in flames, where was my sister's body?

At first I wanted to believe that there had to be a better outcome, she had to still be alive. However the more I read, the more I started to believe that it had to be true, knowing how my life had gone so far I don't know why I thought it would have been any different now. I felt I should cry but nothing came out, I just sat down staring at the photocopy in my hand.

"I'm sorry Anni."

Bryan said, resting his hand on my shoulder before sitting next to me, his presence was a comfort.

"It's fine, it's not your fault. Did he find out about the second key?"

I asked. It had to be somewhere yet Bryan knew nothing as of yet, we needed to speak with Chrissy and fast.

Bryan agreed to keep digging for me, in all of the commotion I had forgotten to tell him the events of my day. Although, now with all of this coming fourth out of the woodworks, I didn't really feel it was a relevant discussion anymore. I put it to the back of my mind. Life was getting rather complicated of late, I can't say I prefer any part of the days leading up to this moment aside from the good memories I shared with Bryan.

Even my relationship had been tarnished with the sins of my past, there was certainly no going back; but as to how I move forward into the unknown was also a dilemma in itself. I barely slept that night just thinking of how to move forward knowing that I had a sister that I would never meet, I had to find out more about her death and why she died the way she did.

I just couldn't swallow the whole accidental death scenario after all I had witnessed in my life, I had wished every night of my life after my adoptive parents were murdered that I had been murdered in their place. Now I would give anything to trade places with my sister so that she could be alive instead of me, what a life to have lived; one with violence and rape being my everyday living situation.

She died an innocent young teenager in a blaze of flames engulfing her, a frightened young helpless girl been burnt alive in a place she had thought that she could call home. The world was a cruel and dire place with only one light that shined brightly giving me hope, Bryan was my ray of sunshine and now this tiny thing grew inside of me giving me such hope for my future.

Before I knew it the morning had arrived, I felt like I hadn't slept a wink but I must have dozed off at some point. Bryan was already awake and leaving the house, I was on a late shift again so I could go back to sleep if I wanted to but somehow sleep was the last thing on my mind. After saying our goodbyes I went back through all of the evidence so far, I must have read Chrissy's note over a hundred times. An idea came to me, what if Mr Hounslow wasn't a name, what if it was a number?

I looked at my telephone, there were letters alongside the numbers of the telephone, I dialled each number in turn for each letter. It went as follows; six, seven, four, six, eight, six, seven, five, six then finally nine. The phone started ringing, I waited while my heart began beating faster than I cared to admit. I felt as though it may beat straight out of my chest if I let it.

"Hello, Chrissy? This is Anika."

I bellowed through the phone, hoping to God that I hadn't just dialled a complete stranger's number, relief washed over me when a familiar voice spoke.

"Took you long enough to break my code."

She replied, to which I quickly replied.

"I am so glad that I finally got a hold of you, I can't find the second key, my sister died in a fire when she was young. Do you think it could have been with her when she died?"

I asked. Chrissy shushed me through the phone.

"Look it isn't safe to talk on the phone, let's meet in person."

She said. Was the reply that I received, we arranged to meet up in a place not far from me.

I quickly grabbed my stuff and headed over to her current place of residence, it was a pokey little motel on the outskirts of town. I wasn't sure why she was acting so paranoid, however it looks like I was about to find out. I knocked on the door in a code like she had suggested, one knock then two and finally another three knocks.

I waited for a moment before hearing several latches being opened up on the other side of the door. She only opened it a crack before pulling me into her room, after locking all of the latches she sat after making sure all of her curtains were thoroughly shut up tight.

"Are you absolutely certain nobody followed you here?"

She asked, I had taken a cab and parked around the corner like she had suggested before walking the final distance to reach her motel.

"No I am certain nobody was following me, I followed your instructions to the letter."

I confirmed. This didn't stop her fluttering the curtains just to make sure nobody was lurking around the corner watching us.

"What did you want to tell me Chrissy?"

I asked. She finally settled down onto her bed.

The room was dimly lit so I sat next to her in order to see her properly.

"Your sister didn't die in that fire, she started the fire, the newspaper didn't want to shame the Townsend name. They had a daughter but they also adopted your sister, as far as I can tell your family were a big deal which is why they were killed."

She revealed. I was a little confused and felt the need to speak up.

"You mean my adoptive parents? They were just ordinary people."

I queried. Chrissy shook her head vigorously at me.

"No I mean your real parents, they were murdered because of who they were. I hadn't quite got to the bottom of why they were such a big deal yet, however I know for a fact that your sister is alive and well. She was the one who stole the documents, I saw the matching key around her neck. It slipped out when she grabbed hold of me to threaten me, she wasn't aware of a second key seeing as she didn't ask about it. She did however take all of the evidence files with her, including pictures of her when she was a bit older. The only photo's I managed to keep hold of had been in a separate location in my office, I wasn't sure if she would get to you so I coded it incase she got a hold of it."

Chrissy informed me. This was sounding more and more complicated by the minute.

"Why is my sister trying to stop me finding out about her?"

I asked. Chrissy seemed very on edge throughout the entire conversation especially after revealing what she knew.

"As far as I can tell she wants whatever is inside the deposit box, she was very interested in what I knew about it. Perhaps there is something of worth inside of it and she doesn't want to share it with you. All I know is that your sister is a very dangerous woman, she held a gun up to my temple and threatened my life if I crossed her. I have been hiding out ever since I sent you those pictures."

She said. I couldn't imagine who this person was but she was no sister of mine, how could she burn a house down with her adoptive family inside of it?

Chrissy was very keen for me to leave after she had told me what she knew, I had one last question to ask her before leaving.

"Why did you risk your life to help me?"

I asked. Chrissy looked at me with a sincere expression.

"The way Bryan talked about you in his AA meetings, with such love and affection, he made me believe in love again. Plus everyone deserves to know who they are and where they came from, don't you think"

She revealed. What AA meetings? Before I could question her more she had shoved me out of the door locking it tightly behind me, since when did Bryan attend AA meetings? What secrets was he hiding from me? Where was my sister now? So many questions, I had gone there for answers however ended up more confused than ever.

Chapter Twenty-Two

By the time I reached home it was practically time to get ready for work, unsurprisingly there was a knock at my door just before I was about to leave the house. Gabriela had decided to pick me up and take me to work, normally I would want to know why she had taken it upon herself to always be there when I needed help. Whether she knew it or not she had helped me a lot, I should be grateful but I couldn't help but feel there were strings attached.

"Gabriela, such a surprise to see you. Shall we go?"

I asked cheerily. She was a little taken aback by my lack of awkwardness upon seeing her, I locked up the door without allowing her so much as a glimpse inside of my flat. I felt a little violated thinking that she may have been the one to take my photo, if it wasn't her than this lady claiming to be my sister might have broken in just to steal it.

"In a hurry today, are you Anni?"

Gabriela asked as she chased after me down the stairs.

"Not at all, just eager to get to work. In fact I was hoping for some information about Mindy and Bill."

I replied, stopping once I had finally reached her car turning around to face her slightly curious face.

"What did you want to know about them?"

She asked. We both got into the car.

"How long have they been dating?"

I asked. Gabriela started fastening her seatbelt so I decided to do the same.

"Well, for ages now, they even have a couple of sprogs."

She revealed. I was confused, Mindy can't be married to him surely?

"Are they married?"

I queried. Gabriela laughed outrageously, it was weirdly nice to hear her joyous laugh yet again.

"Yes, I believe so, I assume all of these questions are leading somewhere."

She queried right back. Even with her prompting me to tell her what was going on I felt cautious of how I said it.

"Let's say that I know something about Bill, perhaps that he may have frequented a seedy club at one point over five years ago. Should I tell her?"

I asked. Gabriela's face turned to steel as her smile disappeared, I felt in that moment I should have possibly kept this to myself.

"My advice to you Anika, keep your mouth shut, that way nothing can come and bite you on your butt."

Gabriela said firmly. She was not messing around, her face was fierce, it was the first time that I became a touch scared of her.

"Okay, I didn't say it was true, I just wondered if I should say anything if it *were* true."

I protested. The car engine was started by an aggressive shift of her hands.

"I didn't bring you to Rosie's Cafe to start any dramas, leave the past in the past where it belongs. People in glass houses Anni!"

She added. It was as if she already knew what I knew, as though she saw into my soul. How much did this woman know about my life already?

"And if I can't keep quiet?"

I asked. Not so much as a glance my way, she just kept driving with fury.

"I faked credentials to get you through the door, you keeping your job is contingent on you being able to stay out of other peoples business whilst being able to keep your secrets to yourself. Answer me one thing Anika, do you like working for Rosie?"

She asked, after a brief but definitely awkward silence. Gabriela obviously knew what my answer would be. I had no idea what lengths she truly went to in order to make me her employee, clearly I had to be careful or I would actually be out on my arse. I shared no reply with her, feeling defeated.

There was clearly no point trying to be noble this late in the game, I did however want to know how she knew things about me that she wouldn't admit to. If I openly confessed that I had been a prostitute from the age of seventeen, than the thought that she knew something about me would be confirmed either way. However, if I did that it would no longer be unspoken; it would be fair game to be spoken about in detail.

I prefered to at least pretend that she didn't know things about my old life, perhaps I was just burying my head in the sand. But, while under the sand I could at least pretend to be out of harm's way.

"Gabriela, why do you want to be my friend?"

I asked. Her anger dissipated as she mulled this over, she glanced at me then back to the road before pulling up into the carpark.

"Look, I saw you working hard in Crosby's, I wanted to steal you for my own personal gain. I

don't know, maybe I felt sorry for you. You're a good waitress, I guess I like to keep a close eye on my investments. I clearly saw some of my sister in you and got carried away. Let's not get any further carried away with the word friend, alright Anika."

She revealed. Her words were a little cold, I had thought perhaps I had been more than just an investment to her. She was the one who had insinuated we were friends in the first place and that I had somehow wronged her.

The way she carried herself around me had me believing perhaps she even cared about what happened to me, I actually felt bad for not being as friendly towards her as I could have been. She had worried me with all the attention, however now I saw the reasoning behind it; perhaps I *had* been a little too paranoid.

"Well now that's cleared up, I guess I should be honest with you. I don't need a close eye on me, I am not going anywhere. I do a good job, you should see that by now. If I promise to keep my nose out of other peoples business I am sure you can promise to back off. I don't think It's a good idea for you to come by and give me lifts anymore."

I said, even I was surprised by the words that had come out of my mouth, I guess I enjoyed the thought that she wanted to be my friend.

All my life I had been used and abused by whoever saw something to gain out of using me, in whatever way they saw fit. Gabriela was just another Ricardo, I was grateful for the upgraded job however I was not happy with how she had gone about it. I opened the car door before storming into work, I heard her call my name as I exited but was not willing to go back.

Chapter Twenty-Three

After work was through I saw Mindy outside smoking a cigarette, I paused to look at her before walking away.

"Yo, new girl, come smoke with me."

She shouted, I turned back towards her without moving forward.

"I don't smoke, sorry."

I replied. Mindy eyed me up and down.

"Do you think you are better than me?"

She asked. I was unsure as to why she was asking me this strange question, did she know about Bill and I? I stepped a couple of steps forward before speaking.

"Why would you think that?"

I asked. She shrugged her shoulders before focusing back on her smoking.

"You don't talk to me much, that's all."

She replied, I moved in closer whilst trying to be downwind of the smoke billowing from her mouth.

"I just got the impression you didn't like me."

I answered honestly. She snickered at me.

"You're okay, for a new girl. I mean you pull your weight despite the bump."

She said. I smiled at her, she didn't seem as grizzly as the girls had described her.

"How's married life with your new hubby treating ya?"

She asked as she dropped the end of the cigarette to the floor, before squishing it with her foot; all the while grabbing another out to smoke.

"Oh, you know, you're married aren't you? You should know how it is."

I replied, trying to act completely normal about the fact I was mentioning her marital status. She began eyeing me up and down again, I felt as though this was one of the times that Gabriela's words rang true. Keeping my mouth shut may have been a better option than speaking out of turn.

"I hope to God your marriage is nothing like mine, Bill is a dirty rotten no good drunk who loves hooker bars. I love him, but no one else ever could."

She openly admitted to me. It shocked me to hear her words, she knows he likes hookers yet still stayed with him.

While sleeping with all of the married men and perverts back when I was Angel I had always assumed that their wives would be none the wiser, here was one of my ex clients wives right in front of me. She was nothing like I had envisioned. She was just like me in many respects, aside from a few obvious differences, strangers could easily think we were a similar type of person.

"Doesn't that upset you? I don't know if I could forgive Bryan for sleeping with a hooker behind my back."

I said. Here I go again, speaking out of turn, what is wrong with me lately? It had to be the pregnancy hormones messing with me, I would never normally give my opinion even when asked.

"Nah, I would much rather he get all that freaky sex stuff with the whores than with me. If he cheated with a real girl than I would be pissed, sure. But these sluts on poles can't compare to me, he would never leave me for trash like that. You can't expect men to stay faithful when whores are around every corner."

She said. Her words cut deep yet I maintained what little dignity I had left. If I had wanted to come clean about things with her before, I certainly didn't now.

She clearly didn't think much of the likes of me, or at least who I used to be. It was as if she saw us as barely even human, freaks of nature that chose the horrible life we led, I certainly did not choose my part in it all. I just smiled curtly as she finished up and headed back in to finish her shift, after she was way out of sight I headed off to the bus stop.

Gabriela had clearly gotten the message seeing as her car was not in the carpark, I took a bus home instead which was better than having 'an eye kept on me'. I mean the nerve of the girl, she had tried to make me feel guilty for not inviting me to my wedding to only turn around and tell me she was just keeping an eye on me.

I arrived home just in time to catch Bryan before he fell asleep, he was climbing into bed as I stepped through the door. I raced to the bedroom so that I could tell him all about Mr Hounslow being a phone number, I typed it into the telephone in order to prove it to him; I dialled it just as I had before yet this time it rang without an answer.

"That's weird, I spoke to her on it today. I went to see her in person, she told me all about my real parents. My sister is still alive, she was responsible for the Townsend fire."

I revealed. Bryan looked at me as if I were having a mental breakdown.

"Look, she probably went out."

Bryan said, he smiled at me as though I were a lame duck. I know Bryan was trying to be helpful, despite the condescending look on his face.

"I spoke to her this morning, she wouldn't go out. She barely let me in, she thought that I was being followed."

I said. I had to go see her, let Bryan see her face to face. I thought about what she had said about his AA meetings, perhaps that would quash his disbelief.

"You attended AA meetings together, that's how you met, right?"

I blurted out. Bryan looked as if he had seen a ghost.

"How did you know that?"

He asked. I know he was tired, so it clearly was not the best time to drop this bombshell on him. He hadn't even seemed all that keen on listening to me, that was before I brought up his unspoken past.

"Chrissy told me, I am sure you can tell me all about it when you are ready. Right now I need you to come with me."

I pleaded. I was secretly hoping he would want to bare his soul to me, however that haunted look in his eye meant it was unlikely I'd ever hear the full story.

"It's late Anni, let's sleep on it and go check on her in the morning. She may call us back. Perhaps she said what she wanted to say and has now changed her number."

He insisted. I hesitantly agreed but did not sleep a wink that night. I wish I could be as optimistic as Bryan seemed, I somehow knew something was wrong.

Chapter Twenty-Four

At the crack of dawn I got dressed whilst forcing Bryan to also get dressed, he wasn't so impressed with being dragged out of bed yet agreed to my demands. After hurrying to his car I gave him strict instructions on how to get to our intended destination. We arrived at the same Motel that I had been to the previous day, I brought Bryan up to the door so that I could do the coded knock like before.

As I knocked on the door it started to move forward unprompted, the chains that had once held it in place had been busted open. Bryan pulled me back away from the door.

"Anni, it's not safe, what if someone is in there?"

Bryan asked, he seemed to be afraid.

"What if she is in trouble?"

I asked, equally afraid of what we might find. Perhaps he was just terrified of going back to prison, he had already been convicted of a crime he had no part in, let alone being present at a real crime scene.

I kicked the door, sending it flying open; I had to know what was waiting inside. Chrissy was there on the floor, lifeless and still, I recognised it instantly from Crystals death. She had overdosed on something, that much was clear, I grabbed a hold of Bryan's hand as he looked upon the same scene as I did.

"It's my fault, she warned me that her life was in danger. I never should have come here, what if me coming here led her to take her own life?"

I asked, hoping to god it wasn't me who was to blame; not again. Bryan pulled me into his shoulder hugging me tightly.

"None of this is your fault, but we need to call the police."

He said. I shook my head, he couldn't be seen here, he had only just been released from prison.

He was a black man with a criminal record, even though he had been found innocent, I wasn't going to risk it. I grabbed his hand dragging him out of there as we left the now deceased Chrissy, thankfully we hadn't entered the room or left any evidence of us going there. I had gotten Bryan to drop us within walking distance as I had before when visiting her. I felt just terrible leaving her there but what else could I do? The Motel cleaners would find her in the morning, hopefully the police would catch her killer.

Once we had reached home again, I updated him on all that she had said bringing us back to the conversation about Bryan having attended AA meetings.

"I didn't have a problem with substance abuse if that is what you're thinking, my company finances and supports people with addiction. We all took it in turns to turn up to the meetings

to show our support, each time we would go to the meetings we would share about our life so that the addicts would feel they could also share their life story. Chrissy was one of those addicts, she had been six years sober now, I employed her in my company to do certain jobs that she was good at. I wanted to give her another chance in life, the reason I said nothing was for the addicts sake not mine. They have the right to remain anonymous which we have to respect, sorry for not telling you before."

He revealed. Here was me, assuming the worst, I ran through every addiction under the sun that he could have had.

I had been to a few AA meetings myself when trying to kick my drug abuse, I had never wanted to take the drugs so was more than willing to quit. However it was a struggle for a couple of years to get clean, still now I have the urge to use when under stress. Luckily for me I'd never learnt how to shoot myself up so had always relied on others to do it for me, somehow not knowing how to be a solo drug user had helped me stay clean.

I fight it with every fibre of my being, I refused to go to that point ever again. Not since I saw Crystal dead from taking too much.

"Chrissy told me that you talked about me in those meetings sometimes, she said that you helped restore her faith in love again."

I replied after some time. Bryan looked a little sad after hearing this, I hugged him tightly.

"She was a good woman, she was really turning her life around. She didn't deserve this, I blame myself for getting her involved."

Bryan said, he was always trying to be the hero, with me and clearly with Chrissy.

"If anyone is to blame it is me for being related to her murderer."

I said, without thinking. Bryan looked confused.

"Chrissy told me that it was my Sister that took the files, it was also my sister who placed a gun to her head in order to threaten her, saying that if she crossed her she was a dead woman."

I revealed. I'm afraid that meeting up with me would be considered 'crossing her'. His face turned to horror as he thought things through.

"I am worried that she might know where we live, I still can't find that missing picture anywhere."

I admitted. Bryan shook his head at me.

"If your sister knew where you lived she would have made you aware of it by now, besides for all we know Chrissy took her own life."

He said. I wasn't so sure about that, but I nodded all the same.

We both wrestled with sleep that night, it was so unsettling to think that my blood relative could be a crazed killer. First she burned down the house of her adoptive family with them still in it, now she potentially murdered Chrissy in cold blood. Bryan assured me he would get his P.I. onto her case in the morning, I was getting fed up of these ridiculous secrets coming out of the woodwork. I hoped that I would never meet my sister, she sounded like bad news.

I had a day off thankfully, due to me having an appointment with my midwife which meant that I wouldn't be working at least. After the night we had I was glad of it, Bryan also took the day off but made sure that his P.I. would look into Chrissy's death for us. We needed some good news after what we had been through lately, luckily the midwife was happy with my progress so far.

We heard the heartbeat of our beautiful baby, I already love the thing growing inside of me yet I hadn't a clue what sex it was or what it would look like. Bryan's face was a wash with love and pride as he stroked my stomach, he gave it a big smooch before we left the doctor's office. By the time we arrived back home there was already a voicemail waiting on our answering machine, the P.I. had an update for us involving Chrissy. Once Bryan had rang him back they spoke for about thirty minutes, he was listening to all of his intel.

Once off of the phone he began to relay it all back to me.

"The body was found in the morning by the cleaners, just as we suspected it would be. Her room had been searched, no fingerprints were found at the scene. The time of death was between one and two in the afternoon, after you met with her. You left her room about twelve. Suicide is suspected however the

damage to the door that we witnessed did cause them some concern, what if someone did this to her?"

He said. He was clearly struggling with this.

"Surely if you were going to take your life you would leave a note or something, there were no needles at the scene yet she overdosed on heroin. She was an alcoholic not a druggy, yet somehow I know the police aren't going to care about that."

I said in reply. Could my sister be capable of such a thing? All I knew was that a suspicious death of someone helping me discover who I really am happened within hours of me visiting her, that alone was enough to cause concern in my opinion.

Bryan was certain that this couldn't have been the way she would kill herself, aside from that there were too many anomalies. Not only did I have to worry about Gabriela bothering me, now I had to worry about Zuzanna trying to barge her way into my life. I missed the lonely days before I found out about the secrets of my past, it was just Bryan and I against the world. When was life going to resemble a form of normality? My biggest concern was for the safety of my child, I would broach the subject of moving out of town once again with Bryan once the dust had settled on his friend's death.

Chapter Twenty-Five

Another month went by in a blink of an eye, no Gabriela, my stomach was definitely increasing in size now. I waddled around Rosie's Café which gained me tons of tips, the customers would ask when I was due which of course was now only ten weeks away. I had completely lost interest in having sex with Bryan, he understood which was nice.

I was always so tired after a long day at work, Rosie had offered to give me shorter shifts any time I was ready. At the moment I had more breaks which was helping a bit, I was on a break at the same time as Rosie today which hardly ever happened. I decided to broach a conversation about Gabriela with her.

"Hey Rosie, you haven't seen Gabriela lately have you? I have tried both her contact numbers but they have been disconnected."

I said. Rosie seemed displeased with me for disturbing her but there was no going back now.

"She's your friend not mine. Why would I have seen her?"

She asked rather aggressively. I was a little bit confused by her reaction.

"You're business partners aren't you?"

I asked inquisitively. Rosie's face had changed from an expression of displeasure into one of complete disgust.

"What on earth gave you that idea? Does it say Gabriela's and Rosie's Cafe somewhere? What nonsense!"

Rosie demanded. Okay, now I was really confused.

"I thought that was why you employed me."

I added. This made Rosie cackle furiously, I hadn't even seen her crack a smile let alone laugh. It was really rather scary, maniacal even.

"Gabriela paid me good money to employ you, why else would I employ a pregnant girl?"

She said so cavalierly. What on earth? Who the hell was Gabriela then?

"So she didn't save your life which meant you owed her and let her into your business? Is she even a nurse."

I queried. Rosie's smile had turned back into a frown by this point.

"Look I have no clue who Gabriela is, she came in one day out of the blue saying she had a great girl to join my staff, offered to compensate me because it was a favour as you were pregnant, however she expressed that you were a damn good waitress. With the kind of money she handed over I assure you, she is not a nurse. Not unless she is selling medical supplies under the counter."

Rosie retorted. With that last nail in the coffin she returned to her office leaving me spinning from all this new information. I was so confused, the last conversation we had she claimed her only interest in me had been as her investment. What was I to her? Although I'm not sure it mattered seeing as she had disappeared after I asked her to leave me alone, now perhaps I would never know who the girl was.

On the way to the bus stop I started to feel some twinges in my stomach, they became quite painful. I started clutching at my stomach making noises, the man standing next to me looked at me briefly before moving four more inches to his right away from me. A wave of pain shot across my stomach which made me shout in pain, the next thing I knew there was a familiar arm trying to help me up. Gabriela of all people was there, yet again, in my hour of need.

As much as I wanted questions answered I also needed her right then, she helped me into her car before saying anything.

"Let's take you into the hospital so they can check you over."

She said. I had no reply to give her just yet, I was in pain while still spiralling from all the information I had heard about her. The doctors eventually got around to seeing me, I had called Bryan on the payphone on the hospital wall. By the time I had reached hospital the pain had stopped, the doctors and nurses checked me all over.

The baby was fine and so was I, they had said it was something called Braxton hicks, they can mimic contractions. Finally when I was alone with Gabriela I spoke.

"Who are you really?"

I asked. She looked at me and smiled.

"A friend of your sister."

She replied. Just then Bryan burst into the examination room.

"Anni, I was so worried about you."

He said. Bryan squeezed me so tight, I could barely breathe.

"I'm okay, nothing to worry about."

I revealed. By the time my eyes fell back onto where Gabriela had been, just moments ago, she was gone.

"Did you see where that lady who was standing beside me went?"

I asked. Bryan shook his head, the Doctor came back in telling me that I was free to go. Gabriela was nowhere to be seen anyway inside or outside of the hospital, Bryan's car was waiting to take me home.

He made me promise to take it easy from now on, I agreed to accept Rosie's offer of shorter shifts until the baby comes.

"Who was the lady next to you, the one you asked about?"

He said. I honestly didn't know how to answer that, I didn't know who she was anymore.

She clearly took the picture from my house, she said she was a friend of my sister yet every word so far out of her mouth had been a lie. Could I really trust that she was my sister's friend? Could I even trust my sister? She was a stranger to me yet I disliked her without ever meeting her.

"Some lady from the bus stop, she helped me get to the hospital. I wanted to thank her, that's why I was looking for her."

I replied. I don't know why I felt the need to lie, perhaps I wanted to know the truth before I told him who she was. Bryan of course believed every word, he never faltered when believing in me.

I couldn't believe what happened the next morning, after next to no sleep there was a loud banging on our front door. Two burly policemen barged through our door nearly squashing Bryan on there way to arrest me. It all happened in such a blur, I followed their every command as they told me to put my hands behind my back.

Bryan promised to meet me down at the station with a lawyer, I knew I should say nothing. It wasn't my first time being arrested, although I had never been pregnant in any prior scenarios between the police and I. I was placed in an interrogation room, I had no clue what this was about. Perhaps another element of my past had caught up with me.

"Where were you between one and two In the afternoon on the fifth of November?"

I refused to answer the grumpy officer until my lawyer was here. I couldn't quite place why that day was relevant, however it seemed important. I was shoved into a cell until my lawyer could be present, Bryan was true to his words when he arrived with the cavalry. The lawyer got himself caught up on my case before asking for a one on one meeting with me, the day they were questioning me about was the day we found Chrissy dead in the Motel.

I told the lawyer I left her alive at around twelve, however without a witness to prove my side of the story it wouldn't help my case. They had found a partial fingerprint on a glass they had kept in storage, originally the death had been ruled a suicide only to be reopened when an anonymous call informed them she was murdered. I was in the system because of my past as a hooker, which of course did not bode well for me. I was mortified, was I going to prison?

I was placed back in the cell until the police were ready to question me again, they asked a lot of questions, some of which my lawyer allowed me to answer while others I was told to remain silent. The lawyer managed to speed up the bail hearing in order to get me out of there quicker, before the evening had arrived the judge had granted me freedom on the conditions that I return for my court date and the bail money was met.

Bryan paid for it and then took me home, I was not considered a flight risk considering I was heavily pregnant.

"You know I didn't do it, right baby?"

I pleaded. Bryan kissed my teary face.

"Of course I do, I know you are not capable of murder. Besides, you trusted me when no one else did, now it's my turn to repay the favour."

His smile was heartwarming in a time like this.

"I lied to you, the girl in the hospital. She wasn't a stranger, she is the lady who got me a job at Rosie's Cafe. I only lied because I found out everything she told me was false, she's not a nurse nor is she Rosie's business partner. I'm not even sure if her name is Gabriela. She told me she was a friend of my sister just before you showed up. Then she disappeared."

I admitted, by this point I was sobbing.

Bryan sat next to me on the sofa with his arm wrapped around me.

"Thank you for telling me, it's okay. I forgive you, shhhh."

Brain said quietly as he stroked my hair. I nestled into his neck, I was terrified for the sake of my baby. I didn't want to give birth in prison, nor did I want to be separated from Bryan again. He assured me over and over again that it was going to be alright. As I replayed the day back in my head I thought each moment through in my mind.

"Gabriela, she was there, just after one... she picked me up in order to take me into work."

Bryan looked confused for a moment.

"She can only be your witness if you can find her, do you know where she could be?"

Bryan asked. I did not know where she was or how to find her, but perhaps we could track her down.

"Leave it to me."

I said. Maybe Rosie would have a way to track her down, I had to try. I could try to use those angel wings to find her, perhaps she was staying at the old polish shop that was now closed. It was worth a try at least.

Chapter Twenty-Six

I had a little time before work so I was determined to check out the old polish shop, Bryan of course refused to let me go alone.

"Tell me again... why are we going to an abandoned, old building?"

Bryan asked me. We had just pulled up outside of the now empty shop. Part of the stores name was missing from the old sign. The windows had been boarded up and firmly sealed, yet the door was barely hanging onto its hinges.

"Gabriela, or whatever she is actually called, gave me an extremely rare and time consuming dessert. It was wrapped up in a paper bag that had this shops name on it."

I said. Bryan still looked confused.

"It's clearly empty Anni, what makes you think she's holed up here."

He asked. I honestly didn't know, it was a long shot.

"She probably isn't but it's worth a try, right?"

I asked. Bryan shrugged in reply.

We made our way out of the vehicle and headed towards the small, run down building. Getting in was easy, the door practically fell away as soon as we pulled it open.

"I could see why someone would hide out here, it has a lot of appeal."

Bryan said whilst adorning his face with a look of amusement.

Sometimes we felt worlds apart, his upper class up bringing meant he didn't really know what it was to go without. Living each day as it came, wondering if you should waste what little food you had left on just being hungry, or to wait for a certain level of starving you could no longer contend with. To him, this place wasn't worthy of his excrement, whereas to someone like me it would have been just fine to spend the night in.

"Well those raccoons look right at home."

I teased back. Two wild raccoons had been fighting over some old pastry before they skittered away, as soon as we entered the building the had scarpered. I was about to give up my search when we entered a back room.

"Look at this."

I said to Bryan. I could see that some baking had been done recently. There was flour and sugar sitting half open on a table, which had been recently cleaned from dust and debris.

"This must have been where the angel wings were made. Gabriela had to have been here to make them."

I said. As we moved closer to the abandoned ingredients Bryan noticed something else.

"There's a blanket here, it looks like someone has been sleeping here."

He said. I grabbed the blanket and inspected it a little closer.

"It has a name embroidered here."

I said. My heart skipped a beat when I saw 'Zofia' sewn into the blanket.

"This is my baby blanket."

I said. Once I'd opened it up it was clear this wasn't large enough to keep a full grown woman warm.

Just then we heard a noise, we ran out of the room in a panicked state thinking we weren't alone.

"It's just a raccoon."

Bryan said, we saw a black and grey tail running out in a hurry.

"Let's get out of here, whoever was here is long gone now."

He added. I agreed with him, but I didn't understand why Gabriela had my baby blanket yet left it here. Whatever the reason I was going to take it home with me, it had my name on it after all.

Bryan dropped me off early to work, before going into work himself. He didn't often give me a lift due to our differing work schedules, so today was a rare treat for me. I went in to see Rosie in order to explain everything, I begged her for any way that I could find Gabriela.

"There may be a way."

Rosie said as she began searching her receipt records for the used cheque that Gabriela had paid her with. Gabriela Townsend, signed as clear as day. I thanked Rosie before leaving again, she agreed to give me a couple of days off. I went to Bryan's work so that he could contact his private eye, it wasn't until I reached his office that it dawned on me.

Townsend, that was the surname of my sisters adoptive parents. Could she be a relative of my sister's adoptive family? Perhaps that's how she met my sister, maybe my sister didn't die in that fire after all. I got into the office after a couple of flights of stairs, I didn't come to his office very much because of that reason; amongst others.

I was busy huffing and puffing when I noticed a young woman exit Bryan's office, she had an attractive yet stern look to her face. She was clearly pregnant yet seemed to be attempting to hide it. I hid out of sight just long enough for Bryan to return to his office. I feigned running into her in order to figure out who she was.

"Oops... sorry. How clumsy of me, I hope the babies are ok."

I said. The woman looked at me curiously

"Are you having twins?"

She asked. I began doubting myself over whether she was actually pregnant. I glanced at her protruding stomach before smiling politely. I decided to play along with her deception. Her firm, British authority carried through her voice.

"Ah, not what I meant. Sorry. It does feel like twins sometimes. How do you know my husband?"

I said. I didn't feel like I had time to waste on pleasantries. She looked a little pale.

"Mr Lambert? Husband? Oh my."

She replied. I gave her a little scowl.

"Sorry, I don't mean to be rude. I can hardly judge."

She said as she gestured to her stomach.

"He's helping me, I'm putting this bastard up for adoption. I'm due to get married soon and can't be responsible for a fatherless child. I'm too well known in England. This company is a sister company to my fathers so I know I can trust them to be discrete. Especially because I'm owed a favour."

She revealed. Every bone in my body wanted to be offended by this woman but I couldn't help but feel sorry for her. I'd met many women like her in my days hiding in the shadows. They were no better than the likes of me. Feeling brave I held my hand out to greet her formally.

"My name is Anika Lambert, nice to meet you."

I said. She let the tips of her fingers touch mine briefly.

"Jean winterberry. I must be off."

She said. I put my hand up to stop her.

"I might be able to help you with your situation, I know some people who also know how to be discrete."

I revealed. I wrote down my number and handed it to her.

She looked a little confused but she took the small piece of paper in my hand and left. As curious as the encounter was, I chose not to mention it to Bryan. I wasn't willing to confess to my part in potentially crossing a line by talking directly to his client. Besides I had bigger fish to fry today.

Chapter Twenty-Seven

Bryan was surprised to see me, I gave him the name I had discovered. Now he had to get his P.I. to investigate, hopefully helping us in finding her. Bryan's office was fairly modest, there were employees draped over their work benches trying to makes sales pitches through a telephone. Others were typing away at their typewriters, everyone looked hard at work as I waddled all the way to Bryan's office.

There were two big enclosed spaces in the office, one was for Bryan while the other was reserved for his business partner. Some might say it was a little risky for a white man to go into business with a black man, yet they managed to make it work. Although his partner was the face of the company not to mention the majority shareholder, Bryan managed the people whilst still earning a good chunk of the profits. Sharing parents was the key factor in their partnership.

The people who adopted Bryan already had an older son, they handed the business to him when they chose to retire. Bryan's step brother was required to give him a job. In this day and age that was a win as far as being a black male was concerned, Bryan worked hard and earned every penny in my opinion. His partner was overseas most of the time drumming up new business for their company, on the other hand Bryan was more hands on with his staff around the office.

I was certain Bryan could run his *own* company, he wasn't convinced. His parents had been close to their maid who had died in child birth, feeling sorry for her son they took him on as their own. They had always kept him at arms length, but made sure he enjoyed the same luxuries in life Ryan had; their actual son. Bryan had wanted for nothing except for his parents love and affection, I'd never met them and Bryan barely spoke about them.

Once we were safe inside his office, with the door closed, I showed Bryan the information I had newly discovered about Gabriela. He was as surprised as I was. He called his P.I. straight away, or at least as soon as I agreed to sit down and rest. He was sure that it wasn't good for the baby, climbing all of those stairs.

"No Ryan today?"

I said. Bryan shook his head whilst sending his receptionist off to fetch us some lunch. Ryan and Bryan Lambert, the unstoppable force of business. The irony over his name practically being an abbreviation of black Ryan was completely lost on my husband.

"No, the partners are having a big meeting so it's all hands on deck."

He said. He was all business as he typed away on his computer.

I love how take charge he became while in his office, I adored the man more than I could ever express.

"Rosie gave me a couple of days off."

I revealed. Bryan was heavily distracted but managed to acknowledge my words briefly.

After having some lunch along with some rest Bryan promised he would update me in the evening, I agreed to go back home so that I could relax and take it easy. Walking to the bus stop I felt a little lost, my life had become so tangled up in all of this mystery and drama.

I was feeling the need for comfort food, there was no better comfort to me than polish pastries. I knew of a nearby store that I had been dying to try out, so off I went without a care in the world. I should have been extremely worried about the situation I had landed myself in, but all I could focus on was that delicious pastry making its way into my stomach.

Upon arriving at the shop I saw one I wanted to try straight away, I ordered it in Polish just like I usually would. I received strange looks from the cashier lady, she kept glancing at me as if I were an alien. I decided to speak in English instead.

"How much do I owe you for this?"

I asked again. The lady seemed to wake up from the trance.

"I understood you, You look just like someone I used to know."

She said, also in English. Although confused by her statement I didn't much wish to engage her in conversation, she had to be at least sixty years of age. I smiled briefly before trying to escape, I didn't get far before she grabbed my wrist.

"You're eyes, they match hers perfectly... Do you know who you look like?"

She asked, continuing to speak in English. I gently shook my head.

"She was a friend of mine, she was pregnant just like you when they ended her life. Dranie."

She said. Dranie was Polish for bastard. Clearly she wasn't a fan of the people who took the life of her friend. Although why would she be, I'm sure I could think of far worse language to use for that kind of evil.

"Tell me, do you know of a lady called Aleksandra Kowalski?"

She asked. Aside from the fact that the lady she had mentioned had the same surname that I had been born with, I couldn't say that the name was familiar to me. I don't know whether it was the impending doom of imprisonment or the sorrow that I saw in the lady's eyes, either way I decided to say something.

"I can't say that I have heard of her, however I did know of a girl called Zofia Kowalski. It was the name I was born with."

I revealed, she gasped in response.

"Can it be?"

She asked. A glimmer had surfaced in her eyes as she began to smile, she started talking in Polish rather fast.

I could barely make out what she was saying, I hadn't spoken fluent Polish since I was eight years old. My adoptive parents would make me speak in English all the time, it was as if they had wanted me to forget altogether that I had been born in Poland. The little that I did pick up was about her excitement over seeing my face once again, did I know this lady somehow?

"You were a beautiful baby, I took good care of you before they split us all up. They took you away from your sister, they said you could forget the life you had and start again. I feared I would never see you again."

© created by Scarlet Rivers 31st January 2018

The lady said. She gave up speaking Polish as soon as she realised I wasn't hearing any of it. The woman began sobbing as she touched my face, I didn't know what to say to her.

"Well it looks like they got their way, I remember nothing. I only found out I was adopted this year."

I said. I paused before asking a question I was scared to ask.

"Why were my parents killed?"

I asked. The shops little bell rang to alert us to an entering customer, after calling someone else out to take over from her she took me into the back.

I found out that Zuzanna was only my half sister, my mother had Zuzanna when she was very young. He was a German army officer, he had been there posing as a tourist when he was actually spying on the country. Germany was due to invade any day while Poland was entirely unaware of this.

She hadn't a care in the world, just as it should be for a young girl of eighteen. She had fallen in love and nothing could keep them apart, however her parents found out she was pregnant which made them set on marrying her off. There was a wealthy widower wanting to marry in the town, her mum made all the arrangements however my mother was determined to marry for love. She tried to track down the German army officer, yet he only shunned her, denying he had ever touched her.

Heartbroken she returned to Poland, knowing she would have to marry the widower. It was as if destiny smiled on her as she sat down at the train station. She had been quietly sobbing to herself when this handsome young man stopped in order to see what could be wrong, he even dried her tears away.

You could tell from the first glance that this man had come from greatness, she told him her sad tale. He refused to let her meet such a sad ending, he whisked her away to his place a residence. He was a duke descended from the monarch who used to rule Poland, unfortunately few had survived after the monarchy had been abolished in 1918.

They kept themselves well hidden and out of harm's way trying to live normal lives. He of course sympathised to her plight seeing as it was a similar one to his, it wasn't long before they were married. They lived a fruitful life, happily married for nearly ten years. They had virtually forgotten why they had gone into hiding all of those years ago until some rebels discovered him. He had taken my mother on a trip into the town while the lady who now owned this shop watched over us, her name was Agata as I found out while deep into conversation with her.

My father's name was Franciszek, unfortunately for him he looked just like his ancestors. Someone recognised him while out shopping, my mother was eight months pregnant with what they were sure was going to be my brother. My mother had tried to stop them but that only led to her being taken as well, they dragged them to an alleyway before shooting them both in the head. There were a lot of enemies of the old monarchy and unfortunately that has led to the untimely demise of my parents. Their driver had gone searching for them only to find their lifeless bodies, it was no longer safe for us to be living where we were.

Zuzanna was placed with a respectable English family in order to protect her, her life was in more danger considering she had German blood flowing through her veins. I was young enough to forget who I was, which was exactly what happened; I was left with a young couple who couldn't have kids. The records of my parents existence were purged in order to keep us safe, although after telling Agata what happened to my sister and I she began sobbing uncontrollably.

As much as I tried to reassure her that she did her best, this only made her more upset. Time had run away from me while talking with Agata, it had gotten dark outside. I promised to come back and visit her again soon, she accepted that I had to leave. I was glad to know a bit more about myself, yet just as sad to hear the unhappy ending my parents had.

Chapter Twenty-Eight

Bryan was waiting for me when I got home, he was not in the best of moods with me. Not that I blamed him, I did kind of go AWOL.

"Where on earth have you been?I have been worried sick!"

He demanded. I hadn't really seen this side of him before, it was nice to know he cared so much.

"I'm really sorry, I have so much to catch you up on. I know how my parents died."

I revealed. After allowing him a few minutes to calm down, he then became more willing to listen to what I had discovered.

I relayed the whole horrific tale to him just as Agata had to me, although I suppose I rushed through it a tad faster than she had. Bryan sat down on the sofa looking bewildered, I decided to join him. It felt good to finally rest my feet.

"Well I ran into somewhat of a dead end when it came to Gabriela, Gabriela Townsend was the name of a girl who in theory died in a fire. Your sister's adoptive parents never went on record with the adoption, Gabriela was the name of their own daughter. Although the strange thing is that no death certificate could be found for Gabriela Townsend or Zuzanna Kowalski, three bodies were discovered in the fire. Gabriela is only presumed dead, but as to who this lady you have met is I have no clue where she might be."

Bryan revealed. I was a little disheartened to find out this new information, who was this woman to me?

Gabriela was my only life line yet I had no way of contacting her, she only ever appeared when I needed help. However that thought had given me an idea, perhaps if I put myself in trouble or some sort of danger she would show up like she had done in the past. Bryan did not like the sound of me putting myself deliberately in harm's way, I on the other hand saw no other choice.

Now I just had to decide in what way I could endanger myself, just enough to draw her out all without Bryan ever finding out. I thought about when she had showed up out of the blue, back when I had been having Braxton hicks by the bus stop. Perhaps I could try and recreate that moment, although she might not go for it so easily. Without Bryan's consent I decided to try it tomorrow, what did I honestly have to lose?

The next day did not go to plan, it was as if Bryan had read my mind. He decided to take a day off of work so that he could stay home with me, he said that if I could take a day off then so could he. As much as I enjoyed the time at home with him, I also really wanted to try and find Gabriela. Did my sister murder her adoptive family then steal her adoptive sister's name? Was my sister a thief as well as a killer? Was Gabriela my sister?

All these questions filled my mind, none of them having any answers. Either way she was my only witness that could prove I was not a murderer, moreover if she was my sister would she even be trustworthy? She had lied about everything so far, however at least I would know my sister hadn't killed Chrissy.

Gabriela couldn't have been responsible for her death considering that she was with me, but that only led to the question of who was. The more I thought about the situation that I found myself in, the more questions arose; leaving me even more confused. Bryan and I made love that day, it was awkward love making considering the big bump.

We found a way to enjoy each other despite my size, it had been a while since we were intimate with one another. I had been so focused on the issues arising that I had neglected my wifely duties, thankfully Bryan was very understanding of what I was going through. I slept better that night than I had in a long time, perhaps it was exhaustion or even satisfaction that led me to a peaceful dreamless sleep.

Bryan had left by the time I woke up, I must have slept through his goodbye kisses. I headed straight to the bath, I had just settled down into the soapy water when I heard this loud banging coming from my front door. I was aiming to ignore it, if it wasn't for the voice I heard billowing through the front door I might have succeeded. As I heard Gabriela's voice in my ears I could not get out of the bath fast enough, so much so that I drenched my bathroom tiles.

I quickly grabbed a towel, wrapping it around my body, as I ran dripping wet to unlock the front door.

"You took bloody long enough to answer, although I can see why now."

Gabriela said. I was still in shock that she stood before me in my apartment.

"Well go get dressed Zofia we have much to discuss."

She added. Hearing her call me by that name felt strange, I was more convinced than ever that she had to be my sister.

I rushed getting dressed so much that I nearly left my bedroom with my clothes on inside out, changing it to the right way added a few more minutes to the whole thing. I left the room fully clothed while rubbing my hair with a towel.

"I have been looking for you Gabriela, I even considered walking out in front of moving traffic or faking labour just to get you to show up."

I said. Gabriela laughed that exuberant laugh of hers.

"This is serious, I am in some deep water."

I added. Gabriela gestured for me to sit down, I did so even though I still felt very stressed.

"You *were* in trouble, you aren't now."

She replied. What was she on about?

"I am awaiting trial for murder. I need you to be my witness."

I demanded. She didn't even bat an eyelid.

"You *were* awaiting trial for murder, you aren't now. You're welcome."

Gabriela said as she grabbed a newspaper off of my coffee table, before she put her feet up on that same table and began reading it; as if this conversation was not only over but also completely normal.

"Who are you? Why aren't I awaiting trial?"

I asked. Gabriela carried on reading the paper leaving me to fret alone.

"I already told you, I am a friend of your sister's, and I sorted it. Although I do wish you would stop getting yourself into so much trouble. I tried to stay out of your life yet here I am again bribing police officers to let someone off the hook for murder."

She said. Now what the heck was she talking about?

Was she somehow the reason for Bryan's early release from prison?

"My biggest concern is who it might be getting you into such hot water, did you piss off some dangerous people perhaps?"

She asked. By this point she had returned the newspaper, placing her full attention back onto me.

"I… I… don't know what to say."

I replied. Gabriela looked at me strangely.

"You look different than I had first expected."

She said. She was the hardest person ever to try and have a conversation with, I ask her questions and she answers me in riddles. Which in turn led to me having more questions, only succeeding in confusing me further.

"Look, Anika, I am assuming you would like to know everything there is to know. I would love to update you, however right now I can't share every detail that you might want to be told. I am here to remove the dangers in your life, after that short man kidnapped you I thought that would be the end of the dramas. If it wasn't for that skinny guy releasing you I would have had to get my hands dirty."

Gabriela revealed. Was she there the night I was kidnapped? How long had she been keeping tabs on me?

"I don't know who you are, why you are helping me or if I can trust you."

I said. Gabriela looked a little hurt.

"Anni, it's me Gabby, you know me. I can't tell you anything else yet, but you can trust me. I got your husband out of jail for you, I just got you let off of a murder charge. Is that not enough? Can't we make a truce?"

She asked. I thought about what she was saying to me, perhaps if I played her game I would find out the truth later on. I did need her on my side, if she was telling the truth about getting Bryan out of jail, then I truly didn't want to become her enemy.

"Okay, so long as you *do* tell me the full truth one day, not too long from now."

I demanded. Gabriela agreed to my condition, I wasn't sure if she was going to stick to it yet but I was willing to try it her way.

I wasn't so sure Bryan would like me working with Gabriela, I decided to keep it a secret. Gabriela told me that she would pick a time and place to meet, she said she would bring all of her intel with her. For now I was just going to have to carry on with my life as I normally would have, easier said than done in my opinion.

Bryan could not have been more elated when he discovered that the charges against me had been dropped, I had to act as if it was the first time I was hearing the news. I had practiced my surprised face in the mirror for at least an hour before Bryan came home. Gabriela had purchased me an extra day off. She felt I needed the extra time with all that had gone on, something I wasn't willing to fight her on. I did feel exhausted, my stomach seemed to only increase in size each day.

My new found friend Gabriela promised to get back in touch soon, but first she needed time to discover the route cause of my problems. I guess she just wanted to know I was safe so she could move on with her life. Without much choice I carried on with my day to day life, which mostly was uneventful. Although today I had received contact from a lady I expected not to hear from again.

Chapter Twenty-Nine

I had all but forgotten about my run in with Jean Winterberry until my phone started ringing. To my surprise the pregnant lady in Bryan's office was on the other end Of the call. She wanted to see me. I agreed to meet up with her that day. She seemed a bit hurried. I met up with Jean in Rosies café, she looked as though she could be giving birth any day.

"I'm surprised to hear from you."

I admitted. She looked distressed.

"You said you could help.. with my situation. My fiancé thinks I'm on a gap year from university… finding myself. The adoption fell through at the last minute."

Jean revealed. I could tell she was desperate.

"Of course I can help, I looked into volunteering at the hospital and I know a lady that will be able to help you. On one condition."

I said. She looked confused.

"Let me stay in touch with you, you might not be able to raise this kid but I can make sure you never worry about how they are or if they turned out okay."

I said. Jean thought for a minute.

"Why?"

She asked. I smiled gently.

"I've seen what losing a child can do to a person. I also know what it's like to be raised by a stranger. You don't even have to open the letters. Just give me your address and let me post updates to you."

I said. Jean shook her head.

"I can't give you my address but I can give you a private post box you can send letters to. I can't promise I'll read what you send but I'll allow you to keep me up to date. I set it up for documents I didn't want arriving at my marital home, perhaps I knew this day would come."

She said. I took her to see my friend as soon as I had the address in my hand. The truth was that she was a social worker I knew from my time as a prostitute. I didn't want her to know the ins and outs of how I knew my friend Jillian.

I took Jean to her office, she looked a little on edge as we entered the building.

"Is this social services?"

She asked. I shook my head for a minute.

"It's not what you think."

I confessed. Jean looked as though she might bolt.

"She has an off the books operation, she helps deserving people adopt children, but for some reason or other they have been rejected by the system. Perhaps they didn't earn quite enough or their race and religion were a problem. Sometimes they are considered too old or even too young. Jillian pairs people that want to remain anonymous with parents that can provide a loving home. She can make it look legit without it trailing back to you."

I revealed. Jean inhaled sharply before agreeing to follow me. Often when prostitutes accidentally got pregnant, they would come to her for help finding their baby a good home. Crystal had given up a baby this way when she was only nineteen.

"Hey Jillian."

I whispered and waved to get her attention. She hurried us into her office.

"Hey Anika, so nice to see you. You are looking well."

She said, her face was full of pride. She could tell I had cleaned up my act.

"Thanks, this is my friend Jean."

I said. Jean gently shook the ladies hand before sitting down.

"It just so happens that we have an amazing couple who would be perfect to raise your child. Would you like to meet them?"

Jillian asked. Jean shook her head.

"It's best I know nothing."

She said. I felt a pinch of sadness as she spoke. She was determined to act as though this child never existed.

"I will pay handsomely to make sure the child is well taken care of, but I don't wish to know any details about it or who will raise it."

She said. She pulled a large wad of cash out of her purse.

"Okay, I will make sure the new parents get the money. You will need to give birth to the child and register the baby and I will take care of the transfer of parental rights. I will be there at the

hospital to collect the baby and I promise you will have no contact after that day."

Jillian said. Jean accepted the conditions she proposed.

"Anika is allowed to stay in contact with the new parents, I'd like her to meet with them. I trust her judgement."

She said. These words surprised me through and through. Jillian left us alone so she could get some paperwork set up.

"Why?"

I asked her.

"You want to send me updates, you already seem to care more about this baby than I do. I believe you will make the right decision when it comes to its care providers."

She revealed. I hoped to god that wasn't actually true, surely she cared about the future welfare of her child.

"I'd be honoured."

I said. After Jillian returned we signed some paperwork and Jean took her leave. She would make sure Jillian was contacted when she went into labour.

I met with the Fosters, they were a nice couple. They hadn't earned enough money to fit the criteria of adopting a child. Mrs Foster couldn't have children, so this would be a dream come true. They promised to keep the money aside for important things the baby will need like education or doctor bills. I explained the situation to them and they agreed to the terms Jean had set.

We set up a plan to allow me to visit as a family friend, so long as I didn't have direct contact with the child. They didn't want him confused but were very happy sending me updates and arranging meetings once a year. I was understanding over their terms, I didn't want to impede on their chance to have a happy life with their child. The contract was drawn up and all parties signed it.

So long as Jean didn't change her mind, her baby would grow up as a Foster. I secretly hoped she would change her mind, but it was out of my hands. I updated Bryan about what I had been up to all day. He was surprised I'd kept it from him for so long but was happy that his favour to Jean had been paid off. I was also happy to be in the arms of my loving husband. Our child will always find love in our arms no matter how hard the future may be.

Chapter Thirty

A few weeks went by without any sign of Gabriela, I had nearly given up all hope of seeing her ever again. Perhaps she had only popped up to get me out of trouble, but then why did she come tell me in person. I nearly spilled the beans one night when cuddled up on the sofa with Bryan, yet something held me back. I didn't understand the strange hold that Gabriela had over me. He still thought his lawyer had worked his magic to free me.

I knew Gabriela was trouble yet I couldn't help but be sucked into her plan, some part of me wished that she *was* my sister. I had been left alone to close up

Rosie's Cafe, everyone else was off celebrating Christmas by getting drunk. I wasn't drinking, which meant I had become the designated shop closer for the evening; I was fine with closing up. It's not that I hadn't done it before, I had just never been alone while doing it.

I also had been given the morning open too, with less than three weeks until my due date things took much longer to do. As I turned around to lock up the door, two unwelcome guests entered through it.

"Imagine our surprise to hear that you were descended from a olden day monarchy."

A voice said. Even without seeing the wicked expression that went along with the nasty tone of voice, I would have known it was Ricardo who was speaking to me.

"Pregnancy suits you, Angel."

He said snidely. For some reason I wasn't afraid, I should have been terrified as he hung his hand by his side while tightly clenching his pistol.

The same weapon that had killed my adoptive parents murderer, was now here to exact revenge on me.

"What brings you here Ricardo? Where's your normal henchman Bone Crusher?"

I asked. Ricardo sneered at me.

"Former henchman, he turned soft on account of becoming a father. That's why the oaf wouldn't touch you, this guy don't care even if you were pregnant with his own kid. Ain't that right, Razor-blade."

He said. Ricardo's new ghoulish goon seemed to have a glint in his eye from hearing his own name, he was as big as his predecessor yet still had the look of a hardened criminal.

"Why are you here?"

I asked. Knowing Ricardo like I did I figured I could buy myself some time by getting him to blab his plan, he did love to talk.

"Well, I have tried to put your dickhead boyfriend in prison, he magically gets released. So I get you put in jail, only to find out that yet again the charges have been dropped. I have been racking my brain to figure out who on earth is helping you, I know that black boy ain't got the power to pull those kind of strings."

He said. I had always known deep down that Ricardo had been behind Bryan's arrest, although I had hoped Big Joe was the one.

Now I knew that he was not only Chrissy's murderer, he also framed me just as he did Bryan.

"You killed Crystal too, I recognise the way Chrissy died. All except for the broken locks was the same. Why did you let me go see her knowing you had killed her?"

I asked. Ricardo looked impressed at my ability to put two and two together.

"I figured I'd give you a glimpse into your own future, no one gets out and free from your line of work. Dead hookers do less talking."

He said. I must admit I became the tiniest bit afraid after that statement.

"So why let me go before? What are you going to do to me?"

I asked. I began to feel fear seeping in as I awaited his reply, his grin wasn't helping.

"I guess I had a moment of weakness, you already lost your baby daddy. Now you're back with the black dick you love so much. Besides big boss man wants you out of his way, for good. I am going to kidnap you, hold you for ransom. When that love sick puppy you call a boyfriend pays up, not only will I kill him in front of you, you'll die straight after."

He revealed. Before I had a chance to reply, as if out of nowhere, Gabriela had knocked Ricardo out before shooting Razor-blade in the back of his head, their bodies fell like a sack of potatoes crash landing on the floor.

I noticed that she had used her gun to knock Ricardo out, the gun seemed to fit her like a glove. She was dressed fully in black clothing, even her hands were enclosed in tight black leather gloves. Her hair had been slicked back into a bun, with her makeup making her look so serious. As much as I should have been terrified of her new appearance, I only saw her as my saviour.

I attempted to speak but no words could leave my mouth, she began binding Ricardo's hands together while he was still passed out on the floor.

"You look like you have done this before."

I said. Gabriela winked at me just before slapping Ricardo across his face.

"Who is this guy to you Anni? I need honesty."

She demanded. That was a bit rich coming from her, but I could tell she wasn't messing around.

"The man who killed my adoptive parents in front of me, his name was Big Joe. I called him Diabeł, it means the devil in Polish. He brought

me to a man to teach me how to have sex in a way their customers would appreciate, this is that man. He became my handler, he raped me over and over again for more than a week before declaring me ready for duty. He also killed a good friend of mine, and more recently a close friend of Bryan's too."

I admitted. I had never said those words out loud before now, as I spoke the words out loud the memories of the many times he had forced himself on me flooded back in.

No tears fell, there was only a hollow emptiness inside as I had spoken.

"I will make him pay for every time he laid hands on you, and for your friends lives. What about the dead guy?"

Gabriela asked. I shrugged a little.

"I hadn't seen him before tonight, Ricardo called him Razor-blade. He was just a henchman, Ricardo was the Devils right hand."

I said. After I had finished my sentence Gabriela shot Ricardo in his foot. I didn't even hear the sound of a gunshot as she pulled the trigger. Who was this woman? How did she learn to shoot like that? And most importantly why was she helping me?

Chapter Thirty-One

Ricardo shouted in pain from his wound, the slap hadn't aroused him but this definitely did.

"Who the hell *are* you?"

He asked. Ricardo was his normal vile self upon waking up.

"I'm *your* worst nightmare."

Gabriela said, she sounded scary to me. Ricardo looked at his henchman dead on the floor.

"I am going to give you endless pain, for every time you touched Anika the way you knew you shouldn't have, I am going to bring you into a world of agony you never even knew existed."

Gabriela said. Just as she finished speaking she reached her hand up by his rib cage, without even using a weapon she managed to break three ribs.

"That was just a taste of what I can do to you. Soon you will beg for death, it'll be the only way the searing pain will end. Who is your employer?"

Gabriela asked. Ricardo, whilst screaming in agony, looked terrified.

"I can't tell you that, he will murder my family for betraying him."

Ricardo said. Gabriela mocked him.

"And you think I won't do the same?"

She said. She recited a list of all of the people Ricardo was trying to protect, she knew the names of his wife, kids and closest friends. Gabriela walked to the back of the Café for only a second before returning with some tools. She must have tortured him for over an hour before he was finally ready to speak, she smashed toes, then pulled out teeth and fingernails.

If I wasn't scared of her before I most certainly was now, she didn't even cringe or flinch when harming him. I in no way felt sorry for the guy but it was painful to watch, I had to turn away and hide in the kitchen during most of it. She shot him as soon as she was given the name of his boss, my main concern now was how we were going to get rid of the bodies.

Gabriela rang someone up on the phone, she was speaking in a different language. If I had to guess I would have thought she was speaking in German, or possibly something similar. Within minutes a clean up crew had arrived, removing all evidence of the men ever being there, I locked up as soon as everything was back to how it should be.

Gabriela ushered me to her car, she was going to give me a lift home. Before we went anywhere I just had to ask.

"I gave you honesty tonight, so how about some from you. Who are you?"

I asked. Gabriela took in a deep breath before answering me.

"You know my name, I was the adoptive sister of Zuzanna. She rescued me from that fire before returning in to rescue my parents, unfortunately the flames engulfed her before she could return to me. I ran to my grandparents house, they didn't want my parents name being tarnished for taking in a 'stray' as they liked to call her. They faked my death, it wasn't until they died that I gained access to my inheritance. I made it my mission to find you so that I could repay her kindness to you."

She revealed. I gasped a little, so my sister wasn't a killer, she died a hero. It still didn't explain why she knew how to kill and torture people, but I decided to quit while I was ahead.

"Thank You."

I said, I didn't know what else to say to a woman who had just killed the devil's number one henchman, I could sleep better at night knowing that not only Big Joe but now Ricardo are in their graves where they belong.

"No sweat Anni, like I said, I owe your sister my life."

Gabriela said. I sat in silence for the whole drive home, thankfully Bryan was asleep when I got home which meant he won't have noticed that I was home nearly two hours late.

Chapter Thirty-Two

I had to be up early so all I did that night was go to sleep, for the first time in a long time I slept rather well. Once I had woken up I was pleased to see the handsome face of my husband, the only normal thing in my life was the man before me. I wished that I could tell him all about what happened last night, however I had no clue how to broach the subject with him.

It hurts not being able to share the most important aspects of my life with him. I got up to get dressed when I noticed a wet patch on the bed. Upon further inspection I now realised that the water had come out of me.

"Bryan, I think I'm having the baby."

I announced. He looked up at me with his face like a scared rabbit, he glanced at the damp patch on my clothes and on our bed sheets. He grabbed the hospital bag we had packed before ushering me to the car. He had to be speeding judging by how fast the car was moving, he seemed determined to get me to the hospital at all costs. I was scared because the baby wasn't due for another twenty-three days, what if something was going wrong?

Some pains were starting in my stomach, similar to the Braxton hicks ones I had felt early on in my pregnancy. By the time I was inside the hospital they were getting closer together, the nurse got me into a private room before getting the doctor to check me over. They kept telling me medical terms that I did not understand, words like dilated, cervix and forceps were being thrown around the place.

They were saying that the baby was on its way and I had to get ready to start pushing, I was given a tube to breathe in and out of which eased the pain a little bit. Bryan held my hand telling me that I could do this, the pain was fierce, I heard myself screaming. It was like another person had taken over my body, they were telling me to push.

I closed my eyes squeezing Bryan's hand, using every ounce of strength in my body in order to push. I repeated this a few times, with each push I felt as if an alien was trying to escape my body. An intense blur took over me before it was all finally over, I hurt everywhere but this little thing covered in goo and blood had come out of me.

They cleaned the baby a bit before wrapping its tiny body up in a blanket, the little crying faced blob was brought into my arms by Bryan. His words flooded over me as he told me that I had just given birth to a little girl, I was awash with joy. As much as I thought I had wanted a boy I still felt such happiness upon hearing that I was holding my daughter in my arms.

"What shall we call her?"

Bryan asked. There was no doubt in my mind what this beautiful little girl was going to be called.

"Zuzanna. Zuzanna Aleksandra Lambert."

I announced. This way I could pay tribute to my mother and sister. Bryan smiled before kissing her on the cheek, we had a daughter and she was beautiful.

"Welcome to the world, beautiful Zuzanna."

© created by Scarlet Rivers 31st January 2018

I felt a rush of love and sadness as I welled up hearing Bryan's voice calling what was once my sister's name. A sister I now new was a hero to the bitter end, it was the perfect way to let her memory live on.

I was busy feeding Zuzanna when Jillian stopped by to see me. She was holding a little baby in her arms.

"I brought a friend."

She said. I could see a small knitted, blue hat on the baby's head.

"Meet Brandon Foster."

Jillian said. I was feeling exhausted, yet I still found the energy to smile at his innocent face.

"He was born a day before your little one. Jean is getting ready to leave if you want me to take you to her."

She said. I agreed so Jillian got a nurse to watch the babies. She pushed me in a wheelchair down to Jeans room.

"Leaving so soon."

I said. Jean looked pleased to see me but only briefly. She had refused a wheelchair and was buttoning her coat.

"If you have come to sway my decision you are wasting your time."

She announced. I gave Jillian a look and she knew to give us some privacy.

"I just wanted to wish you well."

I said. Jeans resolve softened a bit.

"Will getting married make you happy?"

© created by Scarlet Rivers 31st January 2018

I asked. Jean sat down on the bed so she could speak with me properly.

"In order to explain that I would have to tell you the whole sordid tale."

She said. I patiently waited for her to do just that.

"The father of the baby, he's promised to another woman. I fell for him and gave in to temptation. So I received my punishment, giving birth to an illegitimate child has certainly set me straight. I care for my fiancé, I do. We are waiting for marriage to have sex, which will allow me time to get my figure back. He has old fashioned values and our marriage will please my parents. I made a choice, I'm sticking to it."

She revealed. I notice how she hadn't answered my question even slightly.

"I'm not as brave as you, I can't just throw caution to the wind and marry whomever I please. Besides my future husband runs in the

same circles as my love so I will get a chance to
see him. I can love him from afar."

Jean said. I felt so bad for her. I decided to offer her
some truth as a reward for her vulnerability.

"Bryan is the brave one, not me. He chose to
not only marry out of his race but out of his
class too. We met in a gentleman's club, he
rescued me from being a lady of the night. He
nearly paid with his life."

I admitted. Jean smiled.

"Your secret is safe with me, so long as mine is
with you. From here on out I don't know you
and won't acknowledge we ever met. But
please know how grateful I am for your help."

She said. Jean handed me an envelope and left me
alone. Jillian came to take me back to my room. I said
goodbye to Jeans son and my dear friend as I held my
daughter tightly in my arms. I would make sure my
daughter never went without. On the envelope was a
wad of cash, a note read as follows.

Look after that baby of yours, she has a mother to be proud of.

JW

It brought tears to my eyes. I would make sure that truer words would never be spoken.

Chapter Thirty-Three

Life had not been easy for Gabriela, as painful as it was to walk away from Anika she knew she had to do it. The name that she had received, from the night where she was torturing Ricardo, was one she had feared for nearly all of her life; there was only one way to stop him coming after Anika. Gabriela would have to face the devil himself and barter for Zofia's soul.

This man was not one to be reasoned with, if you could even call him a man. Promises were made that could not be broken, it was time for Gabriela to face the demons inside once and for all. She glanced at herself in the rear view mirror briefly before setting off, Gabriela was not the young defenseless girl that had once looked back at her long ago.

Gabriela felt bad for lying to Anika, her dear friend. She wanted nothing more than to confess the truth, she wished she could tell her that her name was Zuzanna not Gabriela and that she was her sister. Except telling her this would be selfish, it would only put her in further danger. She got Anika and Bryan a nice house in an accepting neighbourhood so for now they would be safe.

Memories of her past flooded in as if she were watching it on the TV screen, she could still hear the screams of her baby sister as they took Zofia from her arms. Agata had been looking down at her promising everything would be okay, Zofia was her favourite person in the whole world. A fact which didn't even make Zuzanna jealous, she felt exactly the same way about her dear sister.

They had done everything together, until this young Polish couple had taken her away whilst promising to look after her. They told her that once it was safe that Zuzanna could once again be with her, for now she was to go to England with a wealthy couple. They hid her out of sight, she had private tuition in their grand mansion while never seeing the light of day except through a window.

They kept telling her that it was not safe to go outside, she of course would sneak out any chance that she got. Perhaps that was why they eventually found her, maybe it had been her secret outings that had alerted the monster to her presence. She had been outside when the fire had started, the whole mansion ablaze in an orange fury. She had run into the house screaming, finding the real Gabriela she tried to drag her to safety.

Gabriela Townsend had been a good friend to her, she would never replace her real sister but she had come a close second on occasion. Gabriela would sneak Zuzanna treats from the parlour whenever she could get away with it, they would play in secret because her parents would have never allowed their friendship had they have known about it. The Townsend family were very upper class, they were ashamed to admit publicly that they had taken in the daughter of a german spy.

They were paid handsomely for taking her in and educating her, Zuzanna had always regretted not fighting more to stay with her sister. Everyday she wondered what had happened to her, she made herself believe that she was still in Poland happily living a life of ignorance. A fact she so wished had been true.

Some men came to grab Zuzanna as she was trying to drag the body of little Gabriela Townsend out to safety, she kicked and screamed with all her might as she was yet again ripped away from another sister; even if it never had been made official. She was shoved into the back seat of a black car as she sobbed, not that it made any difference, the grand Townsend Mansion still burnt down to the ground with Gabriela inside of it.

Later in life she found out that all three members of the Townsend family had burnt up in the fire, the man responsible was also the man who she shared DNA with. Her so called father had hunted her down, when he discovered that her mother didn't abort the baby like he had insisted he came for her with all that he had. It took him years to find her, as if killing her friend along with her parents wasn't enough he just had to kidnap her too;

at that moment she was actually grateful that Zofia had been safe and not in that fire.

Zuzanna had never considered that her life would turn out so awful, discovering her sister in the predicament that she was in when she first started following her was a shock. At first she had just wanted to see that she was safe and move on, her life had led her down some dark paths and she hadn't wanted to drag her dear innocent younger sister into that horrible life with her.

Zuzanna had found out as an adult that her Father was the real person responsible for her parents deaths, originally they had been informed that rebels had done it who were against the old monarchy. She had gotten into an argument with her Father, he was disappointed in her performance on a job he had sent her on.

She had tried to stand up for herself only to be told that perhaps he should have killed her in the fire instead of taking her in, his original plan was to burn her down to the ground; however she had been outside at the time of the fire. He couldn't bring himself to shoot her in cold blood, so he changed his plan, instead of killing her he wanted to train her.

Training Zuzanna is exactly what he did, she learnt key skills like how to kill someone with every type of weapon or utensil, or torture people for information. After Germany had lost the war her father went into hiding with all of his followers, he had become a very powerful tyrant over time. He had his mini army of soldiers, private land not to mention a steady supply of weapons. He had his hand in everything that was criminal in the country, money laundering, drugs, smuggling, you name it he was involved.

Zuzanna had never been allowed to get involved in the heavy duty stuff considering she was just a woman, she had become one of the best shooters he had yet he would never use her. Herman Roth was the name of this villain, the name struck fear all over Germany, herself included. Herman had decided to call her Heidi after his mother that had passed, she hated that name, in her mind she would always be Zuzanna.

Heidi became strong and fearless, more than her father cared to admit, she pressed him for details of her parents death revealing that the driver was paid to lure them to their deaths. He was also supposed to fetch Zofia but couldn't bring himself to hand over an innocent child to this monster, Herman had made sure that he was tortured and killed for his betrayal.

Eventually he found out where Zofia was hiding but it took him time to be able to enter the country without being caught, he had to plant spies in all areas that he would need access to. After years of plotting her death he ended up tricking Heidi into being the hand that dealt the deathly blow. Herman sent his daughter on a mission to kill her own sister as soon as he realised his spies had failed him.

Heidi soon discovered that the woman she had been sent to kill was her dear sister, she went AWOL as she thought up a plan to save her. Zuzanna made it her mission to track down her sister and ensure her safety, knowing she couldn't walk around using the name

Zuzanna Kowalski or Heidi Roth she decided on Gabriela Townsend. Not only would it not be recognisable to her sister, it would also mean she could pretend to be an English woman now living in America.

One last time her deceased, unofficially adopted sister would help her out, she knew she could never admit to Zofia who she really was. It took her a long time to track Zofia down, she couldn't believe that she was now called Anika. Her main mission was to protect Anika from afar, taking out any of her father's spies who tried to harm her.

Zuzanna had watched Zofia travel around from place to place, first to the diner than to the prison. Some men grabbed Zofia and took her to this abandoned building. Zuzanna's first instinct was to go in gun cocked ready to shoot, instead she waited hoping it wouldn't come to that. She would often visit her in Crosby's diner, she even went as far as to dress like her in order to start up a conversation. Her would be sister Gabriela Townsend had talked about wanting to be a nurse, so it seemed the obvious choice.

Zuzanna's character of Gabriela was a nurse who loved coffee, she even had business cards drafted up. Seeing how dreadful the place Anika was working in had led her to find a new place for her to work; Rosie was more than willing to go along with employing her for enough cash. Cash was something Zuzanna had a lot of, considering the abilities in hacking she had learnt, after evading her father she had gone to the Townsend bank and managed to gain their funds. There was no one left alive after the recent deaths of the grandparents, the money would have just gone back to the government or into some charity.

So Zuzanna did what she had been trained to do and stole the money for herself, it would be enough to keep her away from Herman just long enough to complete the task at hand. Much to her surprise Ricardo had let Anika go that night, perhaps just because he had a soft spot for her or because she had announced her pregnancy. Zuzanna knew at that moment that she had to go get her sister's boyfriend out of prison, he wasn't her first choice for Anika yet she loved him.

Gabriela had looked into the case file of his arrest already, there was a lot of suspicious circumstances around the murder charge. All it took was one bribe to a corrupt judge and he was released that night, Gabriela had decided that same night; she needed to be inserted more into her life in order to protect her better.

Gabriela couldn't have any more instances like her sister's near death in an abandoned building. All of the pieces were nearly in place for Anika to move jobs. In order to make it seem real Gabriela played on her character as the nurse who wanted to help her become a nurse too, she had made it sound so glamorous that day in Crosby's diner. Gabriela knew it wouldn't be long before she'd receive a call about her false offer to get her into nursing; everything had been planned out. Gabriela watched Zofia's every move that she made, she slept in her car most nights but Gabriela was use to that already in her life.

Everything was going so well until Zofia found out about who she really was, some idiots in the prison had recognised her when she had visited Bryan. It seemed to be Anika's curse to be the spitting image of her now deceased mother, her matching birthmark also showed on her forearm which meant she could never hide who she truly was. Gabriela had recognised Zofia's birthmark and her face from the images Herman had handed her. If it wasn't for these defining factors Anika would likely be dead and Herman's plan would have worked.

Gabriela found out all that she could about how Zofia had become Anika, discovering also about her stint as Angel. It horrified her to learn of the deaths of that lovely young couple who had taken Zofia in, it seemed as if it couldn't be a coincidence that both of their adoptive families had been murdered. It wasn't until Anika had gotten herself arrested that she realised that there must be someone behind all of the things that had happened to her sister, she had hoped it wasn't the same man behind her life's problems.

She had tried to keep her away from the truth by taking the evidence and feeding Chrissy bad information, unfortunately nothing worked to deter Anika from discovering the truth. While torturing Ricardo she had found out that not only had her father been behind her parents deaths and her kidnapping, he too was behind the deaths of Anika's adoptive parents too. Ricardo told her all about how Herman paid Big Joe to hunt the family down and kill them all, it was Anika's beauty that had caused him to pause.

He knew she would made them big money in his club, a young virgin, seventeen year old was just perfect for their sordid strip club. Ricardo had fell for her a little bit which is why he had always tried to protect her wherever he could, he had never taken a girls virginity before so she had always held a special place in his heart. He swore he would never have planned to have her killed, he shot Big Joe in hopes to end his tyranny and take over.

Unfortunately he knew nothing about Herman, Ricardo soon discovered the power that this man had when he threatened his family. He came home one night with his daughter in the arms of a stranger, his wife was being held at gunpoint as he entered his house. He begged for their lives, the only way he could get them to leave was to agree that he would continue working for Herman just as Big Joe had been. Ricardo's plan was to get her put in prison so that he could get someone else to do his dirty work, he didn't want to be the one to end her life.

When Gabriela had stepped in to save the day it had led him to resort to kidnapping her and her unborn child, just before he died on the floor of Rosie's Cafe he used his last breath to inform her of the name of his employer. He swore that he would never have actually killed her, he had a plan to kidnap them both so that he could fake their deaths, that way he could help them disappear; he had to make it look good to convince Razor-blade who was working for Herman.

As much as she had wanted to believe him, he was a bad guy at the end of his life; he would have said anything to save his own skin. It wasn't until he begged for death that Gabriela started to believe his tale, his words **'Kill me I deserve it'** seeped out of his unholy mouth to which she replied **'As soon as you give me the name I am after you can get your wish'**. As **'Herman Roth'** exited his mouth the life finally drained away from him, as if that was his last deed here on earth.

Perhaps it would be enough to save him after death, he may well have tried his best to be an honourable criminal late in life. Herman Roth was a name that Gabriela had hoped she would never hear again. In order to keep Anika safe she would have to take the battle away from her, her plan was to go to her father pretending that she was the one to end the life of Zofia Kowalski in hopes that it would get him to stop sending people after her.

Gabriela sadly didn't get the chance of trying to convince her father of anything, he threw her in prison the second she showed her face back in Germany. It was far from a pleasant experience being locked up in his dungeon of a prison, his men tortured her from time to time; she made it seem like they had gotten information out of her but it was only fake information that she had wanted them to believe.

Chapter Thirty-Four

Anika was safe so long as they believed that she had died, Gabriela had even started sobbing, explaining how she died in her arms. They believed her lies and eventually left her alone, she was still in prison and knew already that her father would try and bring her back into the fold. Five years passed by in that hell hole, even without being tortured the place she was being kept was dire. No daylight could be seen, the air was stale and the bed was made of stone.

Guards would shove tasteless porridge and dry bread through her cell door twice a day, they would taunt and tease her saying how the mighty princess had fallen so far. That horrible experience only stirred up her desire to bring the tyrant to his knees, five years was plenty of time to come up with a plan. First she had to escape, Gabriela had all but given up on Herman ever coming down to see her.

All of the escape plans fail unless he was down here in the cells with her, she thought her eyes were deceiving her when she saw the six foot tall old man walk up to her cell; even in his old age he looked fierce. He had to be close to eighty years old at this stage, she had never discovered his real age but knew he was twice her mother's age at least when they met.

Herman Roth was in great shape, he still did training exercises everyday. He was like an unstoppable force of nature, nothing and nobody could stop him; except for Gabriela perhaps. Herman Roth stood before Zuzanna Kowalski with his old army uniform on, he would often put it on as a reminder to his people who he once served, today must have been one of those days.

He would always speak english when speaking with her, she had learnt German fluently but he liked to remind Gabriela that she was not fully German by speaking English only when with her. The conversation between them went a little like this.

"Oh, Heidi, you do disappoint me. I thought I trained you better than this, but look at you now trapped in a cage like a tiny rodent."

He said. She contained her anger as he looked upon Gabriela in disgust.

"I guess you are just too powerful for me Father."

Gabriela replied. His laugh mocked her.

"You are still so much like your mother, she was stubborn too, but look where that got her."

He said. The rage whirled up inside of Gabriela.

"Are you going to murder me just as you did my parents and their unborn child.".

She asked. Herman's wicked grin intensified.

"I did not murder your mother, she is alive and well I assure you. I told you the story a little wrong, I wanted to see what you would do with the information. I did murder your stepfather, I

shot him myself in front of your mother. I took such gratification from witnessing her pained expression over his death, she begged for her life. I took pity on her for the sake of the child, he has grown up to be a strong boy."

He revealed. Venom spilled from the mouth of this man as he spoke, Gabriela couldn't believe what she was hearing.

"I raised him as my own, an eye for an eye. He took my child from me and raised it as his own, it seemed only fitting that I do the same."

Herman said. Gabriela's emotions could not be contained any longer, she grabbed at Herman through the bars pulling him in close to her. The guards went to go help him when he shooed them away, he seemed overly confident that she could do no harm to him.

"Where are they?"

Gabriela asked. He laughed until he felt a blade press into his gut, she whispered 'Let me out or you die'.

He unlocked the cage leading Gabriela to hold the knife to his throat whilst also using him as a shield from gunfire. Herman probably figured she had no way out so it was better he release her then risk being stabbed.

"How long did you hide this knife from me?"

He asked. Gabriela replied snidely.

"Seven years, I hid one in each cell right before I disappeared."

She revealed. By this point it had become clear that Gabriela could have escaped at any point, but she knew she would never see her father again.

"Why hide it for so long, enduring weeks of torture?"

Herman queried. He still hadn't figured his daughter out, that much was clear.

"You trained me too well father, this knife was reserved for only you. I fed you lies too, Anika is alive and well."

She revealed. Gabriela dragged Herman out of the prison area, after threatening to gut him, he agreed to guide her to where her mother was being kept.

Gabriela knocked out her father out by putting him in a sleeper hold, he was out just long enough to get her mother and younger brother to safety. Her original plan was to kill Herman and get out but that had now been changed. Gabriela didn't want the first time that her mother saw her in thirty years to be a moment where she murdered her own father in front of her. Unfortunately this meant that when he woke up that he would again be after her and her sister, Gabriela's first problem to solve was to get her mother and brother out of the country with her.

Of course Herman usually had a plan for everything, the fact that she was able to get out at all worried her. However that was a problem for another day. Gabriela had a safe house in Switzerland, they could lay low there until they could get to Anika; her mother Aleksandra was so happy to see her. Once they had gotten to switzerland it was time to catch up with each other, after a long time discussing the last thirty years with her mother and brother they had all been caught up on one another's life history.

It seemed as though her mother and brother had been treated very well, her only concern was about what

Herman was planning next. Gabriela made sure that they had not been followed before making plans to go to America, she couldn't wait until she could finally introduce Anika to their mother and brother.

It was then that she realised that she couldn't bring her family to America just yet, first she would have to go back and make sure Anika was safe and let her know who she really was. This had definitely put a crinkle into her plan, she still had some contacts in switzerland so she set them both up in a safe house before returning to America.

She couldn't wait to see Anika and the child that she had given birth to, she was an aunty at last. Although once she had seen how happy and settled her life was she became unsure of whether it was the right thing to tell her the truth or not, she followed her for over a month before finally deciding to arrange a way to speak to her. Gabriela saw her with her beautiful daughter, she even watched her walking into the hospital as a nurse. She had never been more proud of her baby sister than in that moment, what had she done?

Zofia's life was finally on track and now she had unleashed a world of hurt onto her, she would have to make sure that she remained safe before her family could be together again. Her only hope was that Anika was willing to speak with her, the last time they spoke she was torturing a man in the neighbouring room. Not the sort of person you would want in your child's life, there was only one way to find out if she would be rejected or not. Gabriela would have to speak to her sister as Zuzanna and confess everything, who knows how she will take the news.

To be continued...

Printed in Great Britain
by Amazon

85366323R10190